MANDARIN
STAKES
E.H. Ward

Tirgearr Publishing

Published by Tirgearr Publishing
Ireland
www.tirgearrpublishing.com

ISBN 978-1-910234-16-7

A CIP catalogue record for this book is
available from the British Library.

Dedication

For J. Delahooke and G. Cook

Prologue

Guanxi: the word that describes the basic dynamic in personalised networks of influence in China, a central idea in Chinese society.

Istanbul. October 2009. 9pm

The restaurant bustled around him as Okan Yildiz forgot his troubles and smiled warmly at his daughter, who was cutting up kofte meatballs for her five-year-old son.

She glanced at him. Returned the grin. "That's better, Father. I haven't seen you look happy in months."

Okan's eyes flickered. "Jockey Club politics, my dear Sinem. It has got under my skin."

"Then step down, Father. Please don't get so stressed. It's bad for your health. You should be enjoying life, family, and your horses." Sinem put down her fork and gripped his meaty hand. "It's what Mother would've wanted."

With his other hand, Okan ruffled his grandson's hair. Winked. Made the boy giggle.

"I know, my dear," he said. "But I still have so much to do for racing in this country. If only they would let me."

Sinem arched her brow. "Then just tell them what to do."

Okan raised his palms. "Please. I am not a dictator, but I wish I could make people see the big picture. They only think about short-term gain."

He sighed and pushed his plate of lamb away. Wiping his mouth and thin, greying moustache, he stared out the window at the Marmara Sea with the faint lights of Prince's Island in the distance.

1

When he was elected President of the Turkish Jockey Club, he had vowed he would do better than his predecessor and invest wisely in the future of Turkish racing. But he knew, then and now, that the jealous in-fighting of the Club might undo him.

In the current dilemma, it was tempting to take the easy option, but he had *never* done that – even as a child in the harsh winters of Eastern Anatolia. No, he would have to do the *right* thing. By the Club and by Turkish owners and breeders.

A chiming in his pocket made him scowl. He pulled out the device and checked the name on the screen. Letting out a sharp breath, he silenced the call and tossed the device on the table. He stared at it. After a few minutes, he stood. His daughter looked surprised.

"I'm sorry, my dear, but I'll have to cut our dinner short. I cannot eat until I settle the matter at hand." He winked at his grandson again. "Grandpa has some work to do, my boy. We have to go."

The boy nodded.

"But, Father!" Sinem protested.

He raised his palms again, a stern look bristling his moustache. "Finish your food, my dear. I'll tell them to bring the car round." He peeled several banknotes from the wad in his pocket, placed them on the table and made for the door, thanking the manager on his way. Outside, he gave the valet his ticket and paced beside the road, punching the numbers on his phone.

The Friday night traffic bustled by on the coast road. An endless river of cars: honking, screeching, roaring. Okan turned his back on them and put a hand over his free ear.

"It's me," he growled into the receiver. "I'm done thinking about it and there's nothing you can do to change my mind… I'll be telling the Board tomorrow… No, not a chance."

He pocketed the device and lit a cigarette. Spinning on his heel, he saw his daughter coming out of the restaurant, hand-in-hand with her son. Okan's face softened with pride, and he relaxed slightly. Out of the corner of his eye, he saw a car approaching. He turned, expecting to see his own black Mercedes pulling up.

Instead, the car mounted the footpath and slammed into him, tossing him over its roof like a rag-doll. He was dead before he hit the tarmac and two other helpless drivers rolled over him.

Sinem's screams cut into the night air.

Inside the restaurant, heads turned. People rubbernecked.

The security camera outside the popular restaurant revealed the car to be a black Renault, reported stolen hours earlier. The police found its smouldering chassis in a Western suburb the following morning.

Two days later, the investigating officer told a distraught Sinem that it was becoming standard practice for joy-riders to destroy all DNA evidence in stolen vehicles. A simple hit-and-run accident by unknown perpetrators. Sinem refused to believe it.

The cop rolled his eyes at her hysterics. He told her there was no evidence to suggest a conspiracy and declared the case closed, sparing himself months of tedious interviews, investigations and paperwork.

The July Racecourse. Newmarket, Suffolk, nine months later

Catherine Fellowes stood beside her trainer and jockey in the winners' enclosure and patted her filly on its neck. Foamy sweat stuck to her hand. The heaving racehorse's nostrils flared as it gulped in massive lungfuls of glorious summer air.

Catherine beamed as the course photographer snapped the scene. After that, the groom led the winner around in small circles while the trainer debriefed the jockey. Catherine listened intently to every detail, batting away tears of joy. It was always nice to have a winner, but having bred this filly at home on her stud made the win extra special. Right now, Catherine felt as she had when her daughter had graduated from University with a First in Classics.

"Mrs. Fellowes," said her trainer. "I'm delighted for you. This is a promising filly with an exciting future."

Catherine felt a lump in her throat. "Thank you so much," she said. She rummaged in her Hermes handbag and produced some folded bills, which she stuffed into the groom's jacket pocket.

"Well done, Roy!"

The spotty young man grinned. "Thanks, Mrs. Fellowes," he said, leading the horse away to the stables for a washdown.

The last race over, spectators flocked towards the exits chattering excitedly about the wins, losses and thrills of another evening's racing at this lovely old track.

Catherine bid her trainer good evening and decided to let the crowds leave. Parched, she went to the owners' bar for a cup of tea. She leaned against the bar, sipping from a cup. Her phone rang. "George, darling!" Her face lit up. "Did you watch it on TV?"

"I certainly did," said her husband. "I've put a bottle of bubbles in the fridge. She could be an Oaks filly next year."

"Oh, let's not get carried away. I'm just glad she won well. It means so much more when we breed them, don't you think?"

"Absolutely!"

"Well, I'll be home soon. I'm just waiting until the crowds leave."

"See you soon, then. Bye."

Catherine finished her tea as a waitress cleared tables and the barman washed glasses.

Half an hour later, she ambled out of the members' enclosure and down the tree-lined path to the owners' car park. She walked parallel to Devil's Dyke, the ancient fortification that ran the length of Newmarket's July Racecourse. As she gazed at the huge mound and cavernous ditch, she wondered which would crumble first: the bank of Roman earth or British horseracing.

She sighed and flicked through the race card. It had been a lovely evening's sport. All in all, a delightful few hours distraction from the British Horseracing Authority and the endless political wrangling. She had expected trouble when she became the first Lady Chairman, but this was worse, much worse.

Her latest proposal had been met with glazed looks or hostile comments. Particularly from those who only thought about their own interests. Still, she had support from her Board and many small breeders around the country. To hell with the others: if they would not see the big picture willingly, then she would have to give them little choice.

Her green Bentley stood alone in the car park. She stuffed the race card in her handbag and pressed the key fob. As the car clicked, she noticed the reflection of a man standing behind her.

She turned to face him. He was small and wiry like a jockey and held a farrier's hammer in his hand.

"Can I help you?" she asked, frowning.

He held her gaze in an icy stare and kicked the tall woman in the knee, bringing her down. She let out a gasp. He swung the hammer with lightning speed. The side of her head exploded. Blood splattered onto the car. He paused, grabbed her handbag, and disappeared into the thick bushes lining the dyke.

Central Beijing, China - September 10th, 2011

The three dark-suited men walked along the eastern bank of Beijing's Central Sea, one of two lakes inside the Chinese Government compound of Zhongnanhai. They had no security detail following them: there was little risk of public interference here. Since the Cultural Revolution, this vast area on the western edge of the Forbidden City had become a private sanctuary for those steering the world's most populous – and soon to be most powerful – nation into the modern era.

The men walked in silence, but the fuzzy din of the teeming city poured over the high walls, invading their tranquillity. The early morning sun inched into the sky and slowly pierced the heavy grey smog. A frigid breeze cut the autumn air, a harbinger of the Beijing winter.

One of the men moved with an unsteady gait, his lacquered-bamboo walking stick clacked rhythmically on the asphalt. Neatly-trimmed, gunmetal-grey hair was oiled to his scalp.

His two companions did not dare walk ahead of him.

The three men stopped under the Pavilion of Water and Cloud, a small structure built on a jetty over the water.

The senior man used his cane to ease himself down onto a cushioned bench. The others sat on either side of him.

"Ah, that's better," said the senior man, pulling up the collar of his overcoat. "If the world only knew how delicate my health is, they would compare me with old Ronald Reagan." He chuckled.

The other two laughed politely with him.

"Oh, they could never do that, Leader. Your body might be failing, but your mind is as focused as ever," said the youngest man, sitting at the left hand of the President.

The Chinese President smiled and patted him on the knee. "Comrade Ling, you will have your time, but right now I need you to be patient and help Comrade Guo guide our country into a new era," said the President. He paused and surveyed a gaggle of geese on the lake. Then he took a breath and turned to the man on his right. "Guo, when I retire in October, I will expect *you* to be my successor. You understand perfectly how the country must develop, and you have the discipline to maintain harmony and prosperity."

"I will be honoured to take office and steer the vessel," said Guo.

Ling pursed his lips.

The President nodded slowly at his successor before returning his gaze to Ling, who hastily mustered a smile.

"You will continue dialogue with the rebellious factions within the Party," said the President. "You will explain the forthcoming changes and instruct them to remain loyal."

Ling nodded, forcing his grin to widen. "But of course, Leader. I have no doubt they will be loyal."

The President shrugged. "Perhaps. But when men become fantastically wealthy, they have a habit of placing their trust in money and giving their loyalty to their fortunes, at the expense of all other things. You will see that they do not become so selfish, or China could easily take what she has permitted them to have."

The grin disappeared. "I shall be honoured to carry out your wishes."

"Then it is settled. I will officially declare my support for both of you at the Liang Hui meeting next March, by which time you will have prepared the Party and People's Congress to receive the news with approval," said the President.

Ling and Guo nodded.

"By March, you will both have completed your diplomatic tour of the globe. Other leaders will feel safe and reassured by you, but you will – as the Europeans say – keep your cards close to your chest."

The two men nodded again.

"And always remember that China calls the shots."

Chapter 1

The Honourable Charles Buckham abandoned his Range Rover in the valet car park, snatching the ticket without looking at the attendant. The gravel crunched under his feet in the bitterly cold, grey morning as he marched along with a disciplined gait that had stayed with him since his army days. He passed the auditorium, walked through the archway that led to the back stables, and made his way through the throngs of people looking at foals. He shook hands as he walked and dished out jovial remarks like a canvassing politician.

Charles was tall and had deep-set, striking blue eyes and looked younger than his 47 years. He had not changed much since his time in the Life Guards and the SAS. After service in the Persian Gulf in 1991 and the Serbian conflict, Charles left the Army in 1997 to come home to Norfolk. He set up a stud farm and bloodstock agency on the family estate at Brockford Hall, in an attempt to save the place from his older brother Jamie's follies – a mission which had changed his wavy blond locks to salt and pepper grey, and thickened his waistline slightly.

Today's principal mission was to unload some useless yearling fillies that belonged to a client of his – Lord Tony Fowler – and then get rid of Tony's useless mares, too. A few years ago, with the bloodstock market at its peak, that would've been easy. Not these days. That was why Charles currently favoured unloading the rubbish in emerging markets. Places where owners were more enthusiastic than shrewd.

He walked down the steep hill to the footbridge and crossed the brook that traversed the stable area. Eventually he stood under a tree in the furthest corner of the complex. He checked his watch and scanned the people.

"Well, boyo? How's tricks?" said a voice behind him, with a heavy Irish accent.

Charles whipped his head around. "Where the devil did you come out of?"

Billy Malone ignored the question and lit a cigarette, inhaling as if it was the elixir of life. His slicked-back thatch of greying hair framed his red complexion. Charles despised him, but Billy had numerous contacts in Russia and the former Soviet republics. Although Charles had made money selling horses to Kazakhstan and Moscow several years ago, they were volatile places and Billy was a suitable middleman.

Billy – sharp with money, lean and hungry-looking – was an excellent judge of a horse and a reasonably successful trainer on the plains of The Curragh in Ireland. His principal owner was Anatoly Rimovich, a former GRU agent who supposedly made his money selling off Cold War armaments to anyone who would buy them – or so Billy would say, after a few drinks.

Charles knew, through his friend Rupert Calcott's contacts, that the rumours were not only true, but merely the tip of the iceberg. He half-expected the roguish Billy to disappear at any time.

Charles flicked his eyes around as he spoke. "I've got four fillies to get rid of, all by Dream Peddler. They're broken and ready. Get me fifty each for them, anything on top of that is yours."

Billy's eyes twinkled. "You're a proper man! What are they like?"

"Backward and useless. They've been well done, though. Andrew and the team at Brockford have them as good as they'll ever look. Can you shift them?"

Billy tossed the butt away and lit another. "I can of course, but Anatoly's getting wise to this kind of thing. Unfortunately, he's learnt a bit about horses."

Charles rolled his eyes. "A little knowledge is a dangerous thing."

"Fockin' tell me about it," said Billy. "Don't worry, though, I've a guy called Kharkov in Georgia. He's six with me in Ireland and another forty out there. He'll be the man."

Billy flicked open his phone. "His younger brother takes care of the horses. Spoilt and clueless," he said, punching the numbers.

"Well, boss? Billy here! How's tricks Dimitri? Grand, grand. Listen, I've found four fillies for you. Absolute beauties. They'll be flyers for you, and then you can breed them. There's a lot of interest in them, but I thought of you. Just what you need, they're by the great Dream Peddler, sure he sires champions all the time… Oh, sure they're for nothing. Seventy-five a piece, sure you'll win that back on them in Dubai, or wherever you want to race them. And that's not including the money you'll take the bookies for! I tell you what, I'll give you an hour to think about it… No, no. They'll be gone if you wait. Rightly so. I'll call you back. They're champions, Dimitri, champions." He stuffed the device into his pocket. "Don't worry Charlie, it's in the bag. These guys're like kids in sweet shops. They want to buy everything, and nothing scares them more than missing out or their friends buying the animals and beating them. Easy money!"

"Good man, Billy," said Charles, briefly shaking his hand. "Call me when you have confirmation. We'll split the money and arrange shipping. Where will they go?"

"I'll bring 'em to my yard for a month, tune 'em up a bit, then it'll be Dubai or Tblisi."

Charles nodded and walked away. His next meeting was in the car park with a Turkish bloodstock agent who would surely be willing to pay twenty a piece for Lord Fowler's clapped-out old mares. Then he would meet Rupert and Piers.

Billy grinned as he watched Charles walk away. "Cocksucker," he muttered, devouring another cigarette. "Oh, but I'd love to get Anatoly to kick the fuck out of the arrogant shite." Then he thought better of it and wondered what he would do with his cut of the deal. He opened his catalogue and sauntered round the corner.

* * *

Charles leaned on a bonnet in the lower car park and checked his watch. Mehmet Silah was always late, but this was ridiculous. He watched people come and go for another five minutes, muttered an obscenity, and walked towards the stables.

Behind him, a heavily accented voice called, "Charles, my brother! Where are you going?"

Charles whipped his head around. "Punctual as always, Mehmet."

Mehmet ignored the dig, grabbed Charles by the shoulders and kissed him on both cheeks. Charles grimaced, feeling Mehmet's stubble grate his face.

Mehmet Silah was a teddy bear of a man, who wore a permanent grin under a bushy moustache with matching eyebrows. He had a four-day stubble and a thick head of jet black hair.

"You wanted to see me?" he said, flicking worry beads through his fingers.

Charles scanned the car park as he spoke. "I've got four old mares that would suit your clients nicely. Here are their pedigrees," he thrust an envelope into Mehmet's hand. "Get me twenty each for them, anything over that is yours."

Mehmet nodded, stuffing the envelope in his catalogue. "I'll have to check they qualify for import."

"I'm sure they do." Charles pulled an executive smile.

Mehmet arched his brow. "Inshallah."

Charles narrowed his eyes.

Mehmet put up a hand. "Charles, my friend. Relax. I'll buy them, but I will have to tread carefully. Those stallions our Jockey Club purchased were overpriced, and the board of directors is being investigated for corruption."

"What are you trying to say, Silah?"

"Oh, nothing, my brother. I just want you to know that I'm not like old Okan. I'm a reasonable man. You can always deal with me."

Charles shook his head slowly. "It was simply awful what happened to him, wasn't it?"

Mehmet shrugged. "I'm sure it was fate." He flicked his beads and hustled his bulk towards the stables.

Charles watched him disappear.

Andrew Dixon observed the nine-month-old foal walk around him in a long sweeping oval. He watched the animal stride out. It moved with a grace and maturity beyond its age. It swung its hips with confidence, stretching its limbs and covering plenty of ground with each stride. More importantly, its hooves touched the ground lightly. Just like an athlete. The colt was well muscled and bright. It flicked its ears inquisitively at the people milling about, but remained calm. When it came to a halt in front of him, Andrew studied the foal's head and eyes. You could tell a great deal about a horse from its eyes and ears. A bit like people really, only Andrew found that horses were rather more honest with their moods and emotions than humans.

Andrew scribbled a few coded notes in his catalogue, snapped it shut, and stared at the foal as it stood in front of him. It lacked a little bit of size and needed all the bone it had in its legs. Still, he reckoned it was balanced enough to make a nice racehorse one day, and would do very well with the right feed and exercise programme. After a good preparation for the yearling sales next October, it would look like a complete athlete.

Andrew marked the horse onto his shortlist as a potential purchase for his boss Charles and his friends Rupert and Piers. Charles loved pinhooking foals; he revelled in the quick turnover of the equine commodity and the profit involved. In private, Charles admitted to Andrew that he didn't have the eye for a horse that he needed. Andrew knew that was the main reason he had been hired as manager of Brockford Hall Stud, but the one percent commission on all profit made was what mattered to Andrew – his wages alone weren't enough to support him and his parents.

Andrew thanked the groom and walked to the next row of stables, nodding and smiling at people he knew, working the crowd as Charles had taught him to do. While people were generally polite, Andrew could often sense the underlying coldness toward him. Noses wrinkled almost imperceptibly, greetings were slightly too formal. The sins of the father… Andrew sighed. Would it ever end?

He approached the consignment of four colt foals offered by a small farm in Yorkshire, all from the first crop of Capital Flight – Charles' stallion, which he owned in partnership with his close friends, Rupert Calcott and Sir Piers Bartholomew. Andrew's heart sank as he inspected the four rabbit-like animals one by one. He hated having to skirt around the obvious; they were awful-looking horses *and* badly raised and prepared. He desperately wanted to tell the farm's owner that he should stop dabbling in breeding racehorses and stick to growing cattle and silage. But if he did that, Charles would have a fit, fire him, and assure him that he would never find another job in the racing world again. So he bit his lip and offered encouraging remarks.

Andrew made notes in his catalogue. So far today, he had seen twenty foals by Capital Flight, and they were all terrible. Not a racehorse among them; they were not even nice products for the sale ring. It was not going to be easy to break the news to the stallion's owners.

As he crossed the footbridge, he could not help but wonder if they were breeding too many mares to these new, unproven sires. Maybe it was time to cut numbers again, or this whole business would end up in the same state of overproduction that helped to cause the crash in 2008.

Then again, he might find himself out of a job.

Andrew stopped on the bridge and stared despondently at the flowing water. His eyes wandered to a groom leaning against a stable door reading the *Racing Post*. Its blaring headline declared: *Government To Sell Tote. Offers now being accepted.* Andrew screwed his face into a frown. The State-controlled Tote was the only betting outlet which put its profits back into racing, whereas the bookies had to be squeezed to grudgingly contribute a pittance in taxes. Prime Minister Edward Brookson had long been making noises about selling off the Tote. Andrew hoped it wouldn't end up in the hands of a bookmaker. He could imagine what would happen to racing's cut of the profits if *that* happened. Still, he knew the Tote needed freshening up. It needed to boost turnover. It needed to poach customers from the bookies. Andrew sighed. He wished people understood that the more they bet with the Tote, the richer racing would get through prize money. Trickle down economics: prize money fed everything else in racing.

His reverie was broken by the sound of hurried footsteps. He felt a hand on his jacket and was about to move when he was shoved, hard, from behind. Caught off balance, Andrew pivoted over the handrail and toppled awkwardly into the ankle deep water, landing flat on his backside. Soaked from the waist down, he sprung up, looking for the culprit. Nobody there. To his horror, he realised his catalogue was wet. He jumped out of the water, sprinted to the nearest toilets and held the catalogue under the hand dryer. After fifteen frantic minutes, he had managed to prevent disaster. Some of his notes had smudged, but he could still read them. Water ran off his jeans, filling his boots and forming a puddle on the floor. Shivering with cold, he locked himself in a cubicle and wrung out his clothes.

As he put the damp garments back on, he heard someone enter. Heavy footsteps stopped right outside the cubicle; Andrew could see polished shoes under the door.

"Dixon, that's you in there, isn't it?"

Jeans in hand, Andrew remained silent and stared at the door. What the hell?

A tarot card was shoved under the door. Astonished, Andrew picked it up: The Fool.

"Why don't you fucking wake up, Dixon! You're working for a cunt," said the voice.

"Excuse me? Who's this?"

"Figure it out, idiot. And get out of that stud, before it's too late." The shoes clicked on the tiles as their wearer made for the exit. Andrew opened the cubicle in time to see a tweed coat disappearing outside. He swore and hurriedly threw his jeans on.

Outside, there were dozens of people milling about, the majority in some kind of tweed. It could be anyone, or none of them.

He frowned, wishing he'd glimpsed the man's face. Then his phone rang: Charles.

"Are you finished yet?"

"Yes, but I need a change of clothes. I'm soaked."

"It's not even raining."

"No, but somebody shoved me into the brook and nearly ruined my catalogue. Then I was accosted in the loo when I was drying off."

"What?"

"Seriously. Some looney called me a fool, you the c-word, and told me to get out of Brockford."

There was a pause on the line, then: "I don't believe it."

"Neither do I."

"Andrew, the world is full of jealous, small-minded people," said Charles sharply. "Who was it? An Irish stallion master jealous of our success?"

"Didn't see him."

"Huh, you're not much use, are you? You'd never have made it at Sandhurst."

"He was definitely English, though – from the accent."

"Alright, well hurry up then. We're in the office." The line went dead.

Andrew squelched through the stable complex, out the lorry exit, up Newmarket High Street and bought some new clothes. A few minutes later, warm and dry, he threw his wet things in his car and walked under the archway to the stables. Billy Malone was approaching. Andrew mustered a smile, "Hi there, Billy, how are you?"

"Spot on, lad. Spot on," he said, shaking Andrew's hand vigorously. He glanced over both shoulders and leaned in, conspiratorially. "Listen, boss, tell Charlie the deal's on. The horses are sold to my Georgian lad, Dimitri Kharkov, but not at the price we discussed." Billy stared into Andrew's eyes, blasting cigarette and whiskey breath at him.

Andrew grimaced, "Sure thing, Billy, I'll tell him that." He knew better than to ask the prices involved; if they weren't mentioned, it meant Charles was asking much more than he promised the horses' owner, Lord Fowler. Billy relaxed his grip on Andrew's hand, whipped around and clamped it onto the shoulder of a young Italian playboy breeder who was walking past them. "Francesco! Come here to me…"

Andrew watched the Irishman at work. He frowned and wondered what drove the man, who was a decent trainer, to behave like a magpie. Billy was a slave to the money, craving every piece of silver.

Then again, am I so different? Andrew wondered. The thought filled him with dismay until he told himself that he was doing it for his parents and, well…

His chiming phone told him Charles was looking for him.

"Have you changed yet?"

"On my way."

The line went dead.

Charles cradled the receiver and returned the phone to the desk. He helped himself to a sandwich and sat on the sofa in the small private office that Sir Piers Bartholomew rented from the sales company.

Piers' rotund figure was thrown in an armchair. He was completely bald, with a crimson complexion from too much port, giving him a jovial appearance that camouflaged his ruthless character. As an only child, he had inherited a baronetcy with 50,000 acres of Scotland. He had a wife and four daughters, 30 horses in training, and the uncreased face of a man who never wanted for anything. Physically, he had let himself go after he left the SAS, but his brain remained sharp. Having grown up wealthy, his mission in life was turning his sizeable fortune into an immense one.

Rupert Calcott sat bolt upright at the desk, swiping at his smartphone. His icy eyes matched his steely grey hair, which was cropped short and immaculately parted. He wore a £5,000 Savile Row suit and was chauffeured in a bulletproof Maybach. He was married, with two sons and several mistresses. When Rupert Calcott left the Army in 1998, he set up a private security company and spent a few years eking out a living in places like Yemen, Liberia and the Congo, before the 9/11 attacks changed everything. Rupert might as well have cracked open a bottle of champagne as he watched the footage of the twin towers crumbling into the Manhattan streets. A month later he took Charles and Piers to dinner at the Ivy to celebrate. Since then, his business had expanded so much that he now had 4,000 men under him, and he rented a large chunk of Piers' Scottish estate as an operations centre and training ground.

Piers was thrilled to be a part of it and delighted with the money he made from rent and shares in the company. Slipstream International had several lucrative contracts in Iraq, Afghanistan, and North Africa. Rupert loved the fact that he helped to control the so-called *war on terror* and ensure the mineral pillaging of the Middle East.

Charles, Rupert and Piers had all met at Eton. They had played rugby and rowed for the school. Even as schoolboys, they possessed the inherent toughness of many of the British aristocracy. It was not so much a stiff upper lip as a stiff backbone and an iron resolve to do whatever it took to preserve one's way of life.

Piers yawned. "Pass me another sandwich, Charlie," he said.

"You're fat enough, old boy," said Rupert.

"Yes, but my mouth is bored."

"Not the only part of you that's bored," said Charles, tossing him a ham roll.

Piers sighed and took a bite. "I'm bloody tired of the Jockey Club. What a bunch of old farts. Had dinner in the Rooms last night, some of them were *still* harping on about the Derby being run on a Saturday. Christ almighty, they're all living in the past, pining for the good old days when they were kings of the sport and things trundled on as they had for 250 years. I mean, how are we ever going to make progress?"

"Get rid of the lot of them, I suppose – and the BHA clowns, and all the other suits," said Rupert with a smirk.

Charles wagged a finger. "Speaking of the BHA, the new chairman Richard Malcolm's a good man. He's our sort of chap."

All three men laughed.

Rupert tapped his smartphone. Read an e-mail. Arched his brow. "According to my sources, Ling Jiao's widely tipped to become the next Chinese vice-president. Apparently, he'll be confirmed next March at their big party pow-wow."

Charles grinned. "Good for him!"

"Hear, hear!" said Piers. "Ling's a proper chap.

Charles opened his mouth as if to speak, but stared blankly at his teacup for a moment.

Rupert caught the look. "Do we still have that thing?" he asked.

Charles blinked and flicked his eyes at Rupert. "It's on a disc, Rupe."

Rupert nodded.

"Keeping up with technology for once, Charlie," said Piers in a dry tone.

"Anyway," said Rupert. "I thought your little dog Dixon was coming?"

"He'll be along in a minute," said Charles, munching a sandwich. "That reminds me; I've slipped a new photo of his father playing golf to my tabloid connection. That should keep Andrew's confidence in check."

Rupert narrowed his eyes. "Charlie, why don't you stop feeding the press negative things about his father? I know it helps you keep him meek and mild, but we have to associate with him in public. It's getting rather embarrassing."

"Look, Rupe, his father ruined everything all by himself. I'm just making sure people won't forget in a hurry," said Charles, grinning. "Besides, I – we – need Andrew. He's an exceptional horseman and perhaps you're forgetting that he made us two hundred grand at the yearling sales on the last batch of pinhooks. It's not easy to find someone so talented with horses and so easily controllable."

"He's right, Rupe," said Piers. "And don't tell me you approve of all the thugs who work for you. Some of those Serbians you've got are glorified terrorists."

Calcott smiled. "Not glorified at all. Just plain terrorists, but *my* terrorist thugs!"

Piers shook with laughter, his bald head turning purple.

* * *

As he approached the door, Andrew braced himself to face the team of three. He heard the laughter as he put his hand on the doorknob. On entering, he saw a red-faced Piers. Rupert Calcott cut the rotund aristocrat a frosty stare and Piers composed himself. Charles smiled warmly.

Andrew glanced at them all in turn and observed it, like he always did: an unspoken bond forged from years of boarding school and the Army.

There was something about Rupert that sent a shiver up Andrew's spine. The cold hard gaze, the taut skin and erect posture that oozed ruthless discipline. He was still agile and fit, he ran the London Marathon every year – ostensibly for charity, but really as PR for his company. Andrew remembered the first time he had looked up the Slipstream website and seen careful photographs of smiling soldiers helping old Iraqi ladies draw water from a well, under the slogan: *Peacefully securing your investments, invested in your peace of mind.*

Andrew was glad he had never served: if that was what it turned you into. He shuddered when he thought of what Rupert might have been capable of in his army days.

"Have a sandwich, sit down," said Charles. "And tell me what you've got for us."

Andrew put a roll in his mouth, sat beside Charles, and flicked open his catalogue.

"I've found a few nice types for pinhooks, all by fashionable sires, and they're lovely individuals. There'll be competition, but if you want to invest the same as last year, we should get seven or eight nice horses," he said, in between bites.

"Excellent," said Charles. "Are any by Capital Flight?"

Andrew swallowed and sucked air through his teeth. "I'm afraid not. Look, er, his foals are a dreadful bunch so far."

"Oh dear," said Piers. "Of course, it's early days yet."

"Yes, but if his first crop don't look good, nobody'll want to buy them and people will lose faith in the sire even before he has a runner, regardless of the large book of mares he covered. And in my experience, foals that look like that rarely turn out to be serious racehorses," said Andrew. "Unless out of sheer luck."

Rupert and Charles exchanged looks. "So we make money covering as many mares as possible for the next couple of years, and unload the horse on the Koreans or Turks before he has a runner?" asked Rupert.

"Or even the Chinese," said Piers, absent-mindedly.

"That would be one way to do it," said Andrew. "But–"

Rupert waved his hand dismissively. "But nothing. We'll have made a fortune on him by then, and your commission keeps your pockets lined, doesn't it? So who gives a damn?"

"Yes, but–"

Charles interrupted him; "I'm just bloody glad that we only sent two of our own mares to him last year." The three ex-soldiers had twenty mares in partnerships of varying percentages: all of them boarded at Brockford.

Piers smirked mischievously, "That's not what your advertising says! *Supporting our stallion* and all that."

"You know that's only bullshit for the punters, Piers. Like I'd ever risk ruining all our mares on unproven stallions. Andrew: pick the four best Capital Flight foals and we'll pump up their prices with our own bids and make sure some mug ends up with them."

Andrew looked at Charles. "What? That's… that's… we've never done that before."

"Well, we're going to do it now," said Charles hastily. "I don't want our stallion dead in the water before we've knocked the next couple of seasons out of him."

"Still, it's a tricky line to cross. Are you sure about this?"

"Do as you're fucking told, Dixon," snapped Rupert, his gaze eating into Andrew.

"Well, there you have it," said Charles. "Be a good chap and let me know your selections as soon as possible."

Andrew nodded. His appetite gone, he put down the remains of his roll. "Um, oh yes, Billy says he's sold the horses on to his Georgian client." He looked at Charles. "Are you sure about this?

I've read about the Kharkov brothers. People say they're gangsters, warlords. We don't want to end up like that guy, what was his name?" he chewed his lip in thought. "You know, got into bed with the mob."

"Don't worry, Andrew," said Charles, brandishing a grin.

"What happened to that chap anyway?" asked Piers.

"Don't know. Disappeared. Witness protection, I suppose," said Andrew.

"Into a bloody hole, more like," said Rupert, nonchalantly fingering his smartphone. "Concrete wellies, I would imagine. Anyway, if I was Billy, I'd be more worried about Anatoly Rimovich."

"The thing is, Billy…" Andrew's smartphone chimed. He checked the screen. "Lord Fowler. I'd better take this."

Charles nodded.

"Lord Fowler, how are you? Yes, yes. Next week. Oh, he's here, would you like to speak to him?" Andrew offered the phone to Charles, who reluctantly took it. He held it as if it was radioactive, exchanged a few words with Fowler and tossed it back to Andrew.

Rupert burst out laughing. "I can't believe you *still* refuse to have one of those things."

Charles grimaced. "You lot are welcome to walk around carrying tracking devices. Smartphones, my arse. Have you read the user agreements for those app things? Might as well put all your personal information on the internet. No, not for me, thanks."

"Not paranoid at all?" said Rupert, with a hint of a smirk.

"Just enough," said Charles, winking. "Just enough."

Andrew looked at his phone and wondered how he would survive without it.

"Do you even use your e-mail? I don't think you've ever sent me one, anyway," said Piers chortling.

"All the time, for work. I'm inundated with messages and stallion enquiries. Certainly don't have time to send junk jokes around like you."

Andrew shot a sideways glance at Charles and wondered when was the last time he had personally replied to a business e-mail.

"I'll have to get you a secure phone, I know someone in America who makes top class units for the government and military. They're not cheap, though," said Rupert.

"No thanks. I get along fine as I am."

Andrew cleared his throat. "Going back to Billy, he says he can't get the prices you wanted."

Charles snapped his head around. "What?"

Andrew shrugged. "That's what he said."

"How much *can* he get?"

"Didn't mention figures."

Charles pursed his lips, then pulled them into a smile. His eyes remained thunderous. "Great. Thanks, Andrew. Well, I suppose you'd better check the rest of the Capital Flight foals and make up a shortlist for the pinhooks. Oh, and don't forget we're having dinner at The Scimitar with Gary Holdsworth this evening."

Andrew nodded and left.

* * *

Charles picked up the desk phone.

"Well, boss!" said Billy, though he could not have known who was calling.

"Hello, Billy. Did you get those nags sold?" Charles barked into the receiver.

"Oh, er, I did of course, Charlie, but he won't go higher than fifty-five a piece, so that'll be forty-five for you."

"I told you I wanted fifty each, you greedy little fucker."

"Jaysus, Charlie, hold onto your hat. I know what you wanted, and I did my best for you. But these guys love to negotiate, makes them feel like hotshot businessmen, not spoiled little shites. I mean, I'm dragging the fucker out at fifty-five; there's no way he'll go higher, and I'm not about to piss him off over your yokes."

Charles was turning red. He clenched his jaw and roared. "Then you take the fucking cut at your end. I told you what I wanted."

"Look, it's hardly worth my time for five grand each, but if you want to unload them somewhere else, off you go."

"Get them sold, Billy. And get my money. I'm not going to tell you again."

He slammed the phone down. "Rupe, is Goran with you?"

A smile curled Rupert's lips. "Goran always travels with me." He cracked his knuckles.

Charles rubbed his temples. "That reminds me, I'm going to give Eddie a shout tomorrow. I've been thinking; *we* should buy the Tote."

"Bloody good idea," said Piers. "Better us than a bookmaker."

"What on earth would we do with it?" asked Rupert.

"We would make it more attractive to punters, get the turnover up, and give more back to racing – directly into the prize money pool. Then everything'll take off from there," said Charles.

"As I said, bloody good idea, but all that takes cash, and lots of it. Where's it all going to come from? And what's our return going to be?"

"I've been thinking about that, too, but we'll need Eddie's help if we're going to pull it off."

"He's busy at Downing Street all week," said Rupert. "But I'm having an informal dinner with him next Friday at Chequers. There'll be nobody else there; he's trying to have a quiet weekend. I'm sure you two would be welcome to join."

"I'm sure you're right. I'll call him," said Charles. "What're you meeting for?"

"I'm angling to get one of the Olympic security contracts."

Piers let out a loud guffaw. "Ha! Your thugs herding people around the stadium. God help us!"

Charles smirked.

"I suppose it would be a sight, wouldn't it," said Rupert in a dry tone. "But no, I think those kind of roles will be rent-a-johnnies or the Met. I was thinking more along the lines of protecting visiting dignitaries, or high-profile athletes. That sort of thing."

"That'll be a bit tame compared to Iraq," said Piers.

"Maybe so, but it'll be good PR. Smiley happy public service and all that. Anyway, what was your idea for the Tote?"

Charles got up and locked the door.

Chapter 2

Beijing, China

L ing Jiao sat in a plush armchair at the enormous bay window and gazed out at the setting sun. It cut a sideways dash through the smog and gave the whole city an orange-grey tint. Forty floors below, Beijing screeched and bustled. Traffic, people and bicycles dashed like ants. Another day was finishing, and the denizens of the metropolis were going home or heading for restaurants.

Ling let out a breath and sipped a rare single-malt whisky. He enjoyed proper Scottish whisky. It helped him to relax and think things through. He took another happy swallow and remembered the first time he had tasted it: many years ago during his time at the Royal Military Academy, Sandhurst. Ling used to sit up at night with another cadet, Piers Bartholomew, discussing ancient military tactics and using a delightful single-malt to lubricate their discussions. Ling and Piers always got on well. Perhaps it was because they both looked slightly goofy in their own ways, and as a result, people usually underestimated them. Since then, Ling had grown to love his own toothy grin. It was perfect camouflage.

Behind him, Ling heard feet descend the stairs from the duplex apartment's top level. His wife glided across the parquet floor and perched her slim, elegant form on a chair. She smoothed the back of her hair, adjusted her jade necklace, and lit a pencil-cigarette, smoking it delicately.

She exhaled a thin plume of smoke. "Do you have anything to use against him?" she asked, in careful, slow Mandarin; not the rapid street dialect of the masses. "To ensure he will remain

24

completely loyal to your future plans?"

Ling threw a downward glance at his shoes and shook his head. "Sadly, no."

"And you are sure that you are quite safe and," she paused, searching for a word. "Insulated?"

"Oh yes. Very sure." An ancient memory flickered across his mind. A long forgotten weekend break from Sandhurst, spent at Brockford Hall.

Chapter 3

Jess Flint stretched out on the window seat of her small north
London flat with her bathrobe pulled tight around her. She
sipped her freshly-blended smoothie and read the broadsheets.
Her muscles tingled from the 100 miles she'd cycled that morning
as training for her next road race.

Draining the tall glass, she tossed the paper on the floor and
moved on to a tabloid. On page two, opposite the regular topless
girl, was a headline and photo that made her wince. She swore and
ambled across the room to find her phone.

She pressed the device to her ear and returned to the window,
staring out at the grey skies.

"Hello, darlin'," she said.

"Hi there, Jess. How's my favourite copper?" said Andrew.

"I'm alright. How 'bout you?"

"At the sales. Assessing a shitload of foals. They're all starting to
look alike. What's up?"

She ran a hand through her jet black hair, still wet from the
shower, and chewed her lip. "Have you seen the papers?"

"Saw the Racing Post headline: Tote for sale."

Jess rolled her eyes. "No, not racing news. The ordinary papers."

"Not this morning, been working since before dawn. Why?"

"There's a photo of your dad playing golf on page two of your
favourite rag under the headline: *FOR F*** SAKE*. I have to say, it
does look like he's still living the high life."

There was silence on the line.

"Andrew, you still there?"

"What? Oh, yes. Shit. I told him not to play. It was only going to be a matter of time before somebody caught him."

"Sorry, I thought you'd want to know."

"No, no. Thanks for calling, Jess."

"Hey, it's been a while since we've had a drink and a natter. I'm going up to Bucks the weekend after next. D'you want to meet up?"

"Yeah, that'd be great. I'm taking that weekend off anyway. The sales circus is finally at an end, so I thought I'd take the car to Silverstone, then go proper racing at Towcester in the afternoon. Might stay the night with Mum and Dad. Where d'you want to meet?"

"Proper racing? You mean steeplechasing, right?"

"That's right!"

"God, it's been ages since I went to the races. Tell you what, I'll meet you there."

"You will? Great!"

"See you later," she smiled, and tossed away the paper.

Jess and Andrew had grown up together. Her parents had worked for Andrew's for 25 years; her mother Gillian was cook-come-housekeeper, her father Bob – a former policeman who lost an ear and two fingers whilst foiling an armed robbery – tended to the garden and had occasional driving duties. Jess and Andrew had been in the same class at the village school before Andrew went off to a private boarding establishment. Bob used to call them *thick as thieves* and during their teenage summer holidays, Andrew taught Jess how to ride. Then she joined the Metropolitan Police Service and Andrew went travelling when he didn't make the officer corps. Life goes on through the changes, she thought, but do we ever escape who we are bred to be?

* * *

When the light faded into dusk and Andrew could no longer look at horses without squinting, he made his way to the bar behind the office complex. He surveyed the room, looking for a spare seat. The place was crowded, buzzing with the excited chatter of the sales. Hopes of big prices, shrewd buys, profit and loss, and which stallions' foals "looked the part".

Andrew bought a beer and pushed his way to a free stool near the back corner. On the way, he smiled, nodded, and shook hands wit'ı clients. Several asked him about Capital Flight's foals. Unsure what to say at first, he came up with, "Give them time and they'll reward you." He was initially pleased with his evasive reply, until he realised he was lying. But if he told everyone the truth, well…

He sipped his beer and shut out the din as he went through his catalogue and scrawled a list on a blank page. There were ten possible pinhooks: he would bid on those for Charles. He selected four Capital Flight foals. He would give their lot numbers to Charles and make himself scarce when they went through the ring.

Andrew pulled the tarot card out of his pocket and inspected it carefully. Was someone trying to send him a message? Why not have a chat instead of shouting under a toilet door? What a nutter. Charles a murderer? He shook his head, placed the card in his catalogue like a bookmark, and examined the crowd. Billy was in a corner on the phone, wearing a look of desperation. His face was crimson and he had a finger stuffed in his free ear. Andrew smiled as he watched Billy get more agitated. Eventually he put the phone away and turned to face the same Italian he had dragged off to look at foals earlier in the day.

The place was full of Billys. Dozens of self-professed *Bloodstock Agents* of varying abilities, all enthusiastically bending the ears of rich men and women in the desperate hope they would get some of their money, or at least become a little richer and more powerful by association.

Andrew grimaced and pinched the bridge of his nose. We're losing sight of what this sport is all about – the horses – as we engage in the interminable struggle to squeeze blood from stones. He drained his beer, feeling sober and upset. He went off to change and steel himself for a night of ego-pampering with Charles and the larger-than-life Gary Holdsworth.

"Oh, I know, I know, I know," boomed Gary, making sure

half the restaurant could hear him. When Charles entertained clients at The Scimitar, he usually requested the private dining room, but he knew Gary loved to be seen and heard.

Four years ago, Rupert had bought the converted rectory on the outskirts of Cambridge. He renamed it, drafted in a Michelin-starred chef, upped prices to keep the riff-raff out, and used it as a discreet location to entertain friends, clients, associates and mistresses. Such was its reputation, people booked four months in advance to get a table. Charles could turn up unannounced and always be sure of a seat.

"I think Capital Flight'll be a top stallion," continued Gary. "But I'm not interested in buying foals. I want yearlings that'll win as two-year-olds at Royal Ascot. I like to win there and I've done well the last two years. I just knew Regal Delight would be an Ascot sort the first time I saw him. What class and quality!"

Charles smiled and topped up Gary's wine glass. "You're absolutely right, Gary. And the six we bought for you this year are flying up the gallop at Brockford. Why don't you come to see them after the sales?"

"I'd love to, but I'm off to Antigua."

"That's a pity, they're going really well. The colts are Group winners, that's for sure." Andrew firmly believed it as he said it.

Gary was the first of Charles' clients that Andrew had bought horses for. That first year, he purchased six cheap yearlings for the notoriously mean Londoner, who owned a cruise ship company. Four had gone on to win minor races. One broke down, and the sixth, Regal Delight, narrowly got up to win the Coventry Stakes on the opening day of the Royal meeting at Ascot. Gary swelled with pride as he accepted the trophy from the Prince of Wales. After that, Andrew's job was secure and Charles gave him full responsibility for the selection of horses. However, Andrew had a feeling that a bad year would see him cast out as quickly as he had been brought in.

"Oh, I know, I know. Or, at least, they'd *better* be Group winners, the prices you're charging me to break and board them," he wagged a finger at Charles. "But seriously, if prize money doesn't improve in the next few years, I'll pull out of England and put all my stock in France. Over there I'd have a fair chance of getting my costs back *and* send runners to Ascot every year," he laughed. Charles and Andrew forced themselves to join in.

Chapter 4

The next morning Andrew was leaning over the white railing surrounding the parade ring. He watched the first ten lots of the day marching laps, waiting for their time in the adjacent auditorium. Crowds dotted the lawns and pavement beside the offices and stables, their breath visible in the icy air. The PA system crackled as the auctioneer announced that the sale would begin in five minutes.

Andrew wandered inside and found a seat up at the back, opposite the area where most people stood to bid. He liked his vantage point, as he could not be jostled by others and he had a perfect view of potential bidders on the floor below. As he looked at their faces, he saw the usual suspects; the professional pinhookers were here in force, like poker players at a big game.

There were stud farm owners and managers, a smattering of trainers, and the advisors of oil-rich sheiks. Teams of foreigners had made their way to Newmarket from as far away as Mongolia and India. There were Italians, Turks, Germans, Libyans and even an American or two. An eclectic gathering, all searching for baby athletes or – like Andrew and the team – pristine commodities to resell at next year's yearling sales. Despite the international presence, these sales lacked the glitzy glamour of the yearling auctions. There were fewer obscenely wealthy men engaging in ego-driven bidding wars; this was predominantly a sale for dealers and speculators.

Andrew chewed his pen, glanced around, and wondered why Billy was not standing with his Italian, or tucked in a corner with his phone clutched to an ear.

31

The first horse appeared and the action commenced.

Nearly an hour later, another foal strode majestically into the ring. Andrew perked up and checked the notes in his catalogue. This quality colt was well put together and athletic, a ball of muscle with long elegant legs and a beautiful action. Andrew had written just three words on the catalogue page: future Usain Bolt.

The auctioneer began his theatrical patter. He started by offering bland compliments about the animal's physique, while glossing over its pedigree. He asked for 20,000 Guineas and when nobody took him up, he gradually dropped the price to 5,000. Mehmet Silah bid five. The auctioneer asked for seven. Andrew waited, started bidding at 25,000 and eventually came out victorious against the Turk at 50,000.

"Sold!" declared the auctioneer, with Shakespearian drama. "To Brockford Bloodstock. Thank you very much."

Fifty thousand was ten times the covering fee that produced this colt. A handsome return for the breeder, but re-sale for a profit would be tough. Andrew didn't care, he knew that if the horse failed to make a profit as a yearling next autumn, Charles and his friends had the means to put the animal in training. He would surely win a race for them.

Andrew allowed himself a half-smile.

The purchase docket was brought to his seat, Andrew signed it and kept the duplicate. Then he called Brockford to tell Terry Smith, the stud groom, to get the lorry over to Newmarket; at least one would be returning to Brockford this evening.

"Right you be, Andrew. I'll send Colin in the lorry first thing after lunch."

"Perfect, Terry."

He was about to hang up, when Terry said, "Did you hear about that Billy Malone?"

"What do you mean?"

"Well, you know my brother John works as a groundsman for Jockey Club Estates?"

Terry was an incorrigible gossip. "Yes," said Andrew, sighing, expecting another longwinded tale.

"Well, he was harrowing Warren Hill gallop before dawn this morning and found old Billy down at the bottom, unconscious by the side of the road. Can you believe it?"

Andrew rolled his eyes, "I can actually, Terry. He's always drinking himself into a state. Probably got lost and passed out."

"No, no. I mean he was beaten unconscious. John said his face was an awful mess and his arm looked broken."

Chapter 5

"Holy cow, Terry! Are you winding me up?"
"God's honest truth."
"Shit." He paused, his mind whirring. "Hit and run?"

"Possible, I s'pose, but John reckons somebody took a knuckleduster to his face. I dunno. Ambulance took 'im straight to Addenbrookes Hospital."

Andrew thought back to yesterday evening and Billy's agitation in the bar. "OK. Thanks for letting me know."

"It wouldn't surprise me if he *was* done over. The dirty beggar's robbed half of Europe and all of Ireland, I should imagine."

"Hmmm."

Andrew bounded up the stairs to the private offices and barged in without knocking. Charles was alone at the desk, watching the sales on the wall-mounted monitor. He gave Andrew a startled look. "Don't you knock anymore?"

"What? Oh, sorry. Hey, we got that nice little colt."

"So I saw. Not cheap."

"Don't sell him. He'll seem a bargain when he wins a group race for you." Andrew chewed his lip, pondering how to continue.

Charles eyed him suspiciously. "Go on then, spit it out."

Andrew had a pained expression on his face as he spoke. "Did you manage to get the deal with Billy finalised?"

Charles sat back, keeping his eyes on the screen. "Oh, that's all taken care of," he said, waving dismissively. "I've a feeling Billy'll come up trumps for us. He always does."

Andrew frowned. "It's just that I heard he's in Addenbrookes as we speak. Terry's brother found him beaten unconscious near Warren Hill gallop."

Charles flicked his gaze to Andrew. "What? Are you sure? Terry's prone to exaggeration, you know."

"Not about something like this."

"Don't you worry about it, Andrew. Billy'll have got what he deserved."

Andrew shot a puzzled look at his boss.

Charles shrugged. "Oh, I suppose Rimovich or the Kharkovs got fed up with his games."

"Well, yeah, I suppose, but…"

Charles inspected Andrew with a narrow gaze. "But what?"

Andrew noticed Charles' right hand had balled into a fist. "So do we look for someone else to take the fillies?"

Charles relaxed his facial muscles and his fist. "Oh no. No need to do that."

An uneasy feeling shot through Andrew.

Charles continued, "I'm sure he got the horses sold. I'll call the hospital later to see if he's been admitted. You just keep your mind on the sales. Oh, and Mehmet Silah said he'll take Fowler's four mares. They all qualify for import to Turkey and he has clients lined up. So, all in all, I'd say we're doing well for his Lordship. You can make up a shortlist of mares to buy next week and give him a call. He said he'd like to come and bid on them in person."

"Sounds good." He handed Charles a folded piece of paper. "Here's the Capital Flight list."

Charles stowed it in his catalogue. "Thanks. I'll take care of this."

"OK," said Andrew, concealing his delight. He got up to leave.

"Oh, by the way, I'm thinking of putting together a syndicate to buy the Tote," said Charles in a blasé tone.

Andrew stopped in his tracks, his jaw agape.

"I'll have dinner with the PM next week and put in an offer," he continued. "But if you should hear any gossip about it, deny everything. OK?"

"Er, sure. My lips are sealed, but does the company have the kind of money to pull it off?"

"That's why I'm putting together a syndicate. Rupert and Piers are in, and we'll see who else. Look, I mean it: not a word. I only told you so you'd know enough to keep quiet and keep your ears open in case anyone else is talking about it." He paused, pursing his lips. "And if you do hear any gossip, be sure to let me know *who* is saying *what*. Is that clear?"

"Crystal."

"Oh, and Holdsworth called me this morning. He wants us to buy him ten two-year-olds at the breeze-up sales in April, but he won't increase the budget. Tight bastard."

"OK," said Andrew as he closed the door.

It was late afternoon when news of Billy's accident spread like wildfire. In the meantime, Terry phoned to say that Billy had his arm in plaster, fifteen stitches in his face, and would be kept in hospital overnight for observation. At Tattersalls sales complex, however, the story grew legs and by the end of trading that day, it was widely understood that he was brain damaged and would never walk again. Andrew listened, but did not contribute. The general consensus seemed to be that it had been a long time coming and was well deserved. Some even reckoned that he'd got off lightly. Meanwhile, a few sharp bloodstock agents wondered if Rimovich or the Kharkovs would be needing new advisors in the near future. Lambs to the slaughter.

As he drove home that night, Andrew's uneasy feeling nagged at him. There was something about Charles' reaction that alarmed him.

The next day he called Addenbrookes Hospital, only to be told by the nurse that Billy Malone had already checked out. He looked up Billy's number in the Horses In Training book and made the call. It rang through to voicemail. Andrew left a message, wishing Billy a speedy recovery and asking him to call back.

The following day Billy returned the call.

"Hi, Billy," said Andrew.

"Well, boyo, what do you want?" said Billy. His voice was slow and slurred.

"How're you doing?"

"You taking the fockin' piss? I'm in agony."

"Yeah, right. Sorry. Look, Billy, I know this is out of the blue, but when you were attacked, did you have any idea who it was?"

The line was silent, then, "Oh, don't worry. Like I told the cops, I don't have a fockin' clue."

"OK, Billy, but—"

"But what? Are you taking the piss?"

"No. Why would I want to do that?"

"Why would you? Ha! That's a good one."

"What?"

"Don't worry about it, Dixon, and don't fockin' call me again." The line went dead.

Fowler's fillies were due to leave the stud for Tblisi in three days. Surely Charles wouldn't have gone so far just to get them sold for inflated prices?

* * *

That evening, Andrew sat in Piers' sales office with Charles, going over lists of mares for sale the following week. Charles stood and stretched. "Time to call it a night, I reckon."

Andrew glanced at his watch and heard his stomach growl. "I'm starving. Think I'll grab dinner in town before I head back to Brockford."

"Well, I'm going to pop into the restaurant here. The sales company is throwing a reception for new buyers. I'll have a sniff around and see if I can get any of them under Brockford's wing."

Andrew's shoulders drooped. "Do you need me?"

"No, no. You head off. Oh, and drop my hat, raincoat and catalogue in my car on your way out, will you?"

Andrew collected the things. "I'll need the valet ticket."

Charles growled and threw him the keys. "It's parked at the bottom of the hill. Bloody valet park was full this morning. Oh, and don't bother bringing the keys back to me at the reception. Just leave them with the secretary at the sale ring entrance. Tell her they're mine."

Andrew made his way out of the office block, across the gravel under the dim orange glow from the sodium light, and down the hill. He picked his way between cars, searching for the distinctive silhouette of Charles' Range Rover. Eventually, he saw it at the bottom by the brook. He pulled out the key and pressed the fob. Ahead of him the car beeped. Andrew opened the passenger door and felt the stickiness. He looked at his hand in the interior light and gasped. His hand was covered in blood.

He dumped the coat and catalogue on the front seat and closed the door. Squinting, he saw that something had been daubed along the whole side of the car. Andrew wiped his hand on the grass and pulled out his phone. Illuminating the display, he walked a full lap of the large SUV. Then a second lap. Then he was able to decipher words. Someone had written *sell at any cost?* On the side of the vehicle. In blood.

Andrew called Charles.

"Don't tell me you can't find the car."

"Oh, I found it alright." He told Charles everything. "Shall I call the police?"

There was silence on the line.

"No. You go on home. I'll come and have a look and decide how I want to handle it."

The line went dead.

Andrew stood staring at the car. He checked the ground around it and the windscreen wipers, just in case there was a tarot card stashed anywhere. No sign of one. He washed his hands in a restroom and drove home. Only then did he realise he'd forgotten to eat. He didn't feel hungry at all.

Chapter 6

Brockford Hall Stud, Thetford, Norfolk - December 3rd, 2011

Andrew rode the quad bike slowly around the laneways as dawn broke over Norfolk. He enjoyed these frosty winter mornings, the first rays of sun made the grass sparkle. He pulled a woolly hat down over his mop of dark hair, inhaled deeply and watched his breath cut through the air. Andrew preferred to make his rounds of the stud on a quad, with nothing between him and his surroundings, whereas Charles always drove. It was not as much fun as riding a horse in a point-to-point, but it would have to do.

Andrew toured the perimeter of the four hundred acre stud, the only remaining grassland of the once-glorious Brockford estate. He glanced over the fence at the fifteen-year-old forest. Some of the trees were finding the windswept Norfolk winter a challenge.

Andrew sighed. Charles' older brother Jamie, the 11th Earl of Royston, had good intentions, but he had no idea how to run a business. He had planted a thousand acres of trees, which Charles insisted rendered the land useless. Jamie then spent another fortune unsuccessfully fighting in court to construct Britain's largest wind farm on another part of the estate. The locals had won their case and Jamie had been forced to sell another four hundred acres to cover costs and find money to re-roof the house. *Broke-ford* the locals now called it. But Andrew liked the old place and he was sure that the successful stallion stud and bloodstock agency he managed with Charles was all that stood between the estate and financial ruin.

He crossed the back avenue and glanced at the imposing Elizabethan mansion. If the stud failed, it would be a pity to see it turned into a hotel or, worse still, a golf club.

He passed the sheltered paddock where the pregnant mares wintered out wearing their waterproof rugs. "Morning, Colin," he called to the assistant stud groom, who was emptying a bag of feed into the pots near the fence line.

"Mornin', Andrew," he said with a grin. "And a t'riffic one it is, too."

"Everything alright, Colin?"

"Perfect, these old girls are snug as bugs in them rugs."

Andrew smiled and continued on. He pulled alongside the yearling barn and walked carefully up the aisleway, scanning left and right at all thirty horses finishing their breakfasts.

All of them had been broken-in and were now cantering around a small all-weather gallop every morning, waiting to be sent off to their trainers. Some had been born and raised here, some Andrew had selected at sales for clients of Charles, and some had been offered for sale, but returned to Brockford without finding a buyer. It was tough work trying to sell a horse these days. A buyer's market.

Breaking-in the yearlings was Andrew's favourite time of the year. He always made room in his schedule to do the daily lunging and long-reining with them, until they were ready to be ridden by guys lighter than him. Andrew missed riding, but not the wasting. He had grown tired of keeping himself seven kilos underweight by twenty-five; now nearly thirty-one, he shuddered at the thought.

Terry Smith, the stud groom, appeared from the tack room. The rosy-cheeked man in his forties had grown up in the area and worked on a Newmarket stud until he moved to Brockford at its inception in 1999. Since Andrew had joined the operation in 2008, Terry had been an invaluable help – even if he was slightly old-fashioned and unable to keep his mouth shut.

It had been Terry who had explained to Andrew about how Charles and Jamie's father, the 10th Earl, had been frustrated at Jamie's inability to understand the running of the estate. The frail old man's frustration turned to utter despair when Jamie came out of the closet and informed his father that the line of succession would not be continuing through him. A month before his death, the 10th Earl arranged for his sons to share control of the estate. And when Jamie lost the wind farm case, Charles realised that he could no longer oversee things from an army base in Hereford. He had returned to Brockford just in time.

"Mornin', Andrew."

"Morning, Terry. I need to see them all outside when you're ready. I don't have time to watch them work. Lord Fowler's coming to see the stallions. He'll want to see his four fillies here, too, before they head off to Billy Malone."

"They'll be ready in a minute."

They walked out of the barn together.

Terry grimaced. "I can't believe you managed to unload Fowler's donkeys.. Did you speak to Billy after his accident?"

Andrew flicked Terry a glance and ignored the question, not wanting to add fuel to the man's fertile mind. "We've done what we can with those horses, but you can't make a silk purse out of a sow's ear. Thing is, he blames our stallions and not his mares. Typical."

The first yearling was paraded. Andrew looked at all thirty horses in rapid succession, noting how they were maturing and developing from skittish, adolescent animals into young athletes. He studied them intently from the moment they came into view. Later, he would discuss them with their prospective trainers and work on finding new owners for those that he could tell would not be good enough to race in Britain.

Nobody liked to hear *their* thoroughbreds were donkeys, but Andrew felt it was better to be straight, rather than give unrealistic expectations. He'd been realistic with Lord Fowler last week when he'd explained that his fillies wouldn't make winners in Britian. Lord Fowler hadn't liked it at all.

Andrew thanked Terry, hopped on the quad and made for the office.

He parked beside Charles' Range Rover and opened the heavy

wooden door to the converted coach-houses which served as the offices and hospitality suite of the stud. It was all old stone, wood panelling and Turkish carpeting. Charles had even taken a few paintings from the mansion, along with an enormous solid silver galleon, which stood on a mahogany table in the reception area. Andrew gazed at it every morning. Charles was proud to proclaim that his father had liberated it from a continental chateau during World War II. Andrew secretly wondered if the descendants of the former owners knew its whereabouts.

"Good morning, Susan," said Andrew to the bespectacled, grey-haired woman who ran the office with military efficiency.

She looked up from her computer. "Ah! Morning. I'm glad you're here. You know his Lordship will be here at noon?"

"Yes. Er..." He noticed the unsettled look on her face. "What's happened?"

"Well, nothing really, but Thierry Lefleur just rang. He wants to look at the stallions at twelve-thirty, meet you and Mr. Buckham, discuss mating plans, and book nominations. He's arriving by helicopter."

"Well, that's not a problem. I'll tell Charles. Is he busy?" said Andrew, pointing at the door to Charles' office.

"On the phone."

Andrew knocked and entered without waiting for a reply.

Charles Buckham was reclining in his leather chair, shouting enthusiastically into a reproduction of a vintage Bakelite telephone. Behind him, mounted on the wall, were a series of group photographs: Charles with his sixth form classmates at Eton; Sandhurst cadets; Life Guards officers; and a group of camouflaged men standing in a desert ravine beside a pair of heavily-laden military Land Rovers. Andrew knew that the same three faces could be found in each photo.

"Look, Richard, *you're* the Chairman. I'm relying on you to keep the British Horseracing Authority on the right path. Whatever you do, *don't* warn him off. He spends a lot of money in this country and if he leaves," Charles bellowed into the receiver. "Well, exactly! I knew I could count on you to see the big picture.

You're the best thing that ever happened to the BHA," he grinned, then listened for a moment. "Yes. Well, sad as it was, if you ask me that was a blessing in disguise. OK. Chat soon, Richard, bye." He slammed down the phone and clapped his hands together.

"It's so refreshing to deal with a BHA chairman who understands what's required of him," he said.

Andrew shrugged. "I always liked Catherine Fellowes, she was a horsewoman."

Charles stiffened. "She was mad as a balloon!"

"Er, OK." Andrew shrugged again as he sat and poured a coffee.

"Anyway. Tony Fowler's on his way. We'll have to break it to him how much we got for his fillies."

"And exactly how much *did* we get for them?"

Charles inspected Andrew with a sneer. "What's it to you?"

Andrew blinked. "Well, nothing. Except we should be on the same page, in case Lord Fowler wants to discuss it with me."

"Fair enough. I told him I'd get him thirty grand a piece for the four fillies, but I could only get twenty six. The mares will go to Turkey. Ten grand each. Understand?"

Andrew nodded.

"And I'm relying on you to convince him over lunch it was those old mares we've flogged to Turkey that were the problem, and not *my* stallions."

"Don't worry, I'll manage that. It's the truth, after all. If he'd listened to me in the first place, he'd have sold them pregnant, carrying those awful fillies, two years ago. Oh, and Susan just told me Thierry Lefleur is on his way. We'd better include him in lunch."

"I agree. He's right in there with those new Qataris."

"And don't forget Lefleur and his clients sent us forty-six mares last year. I'd say he deserves the red carpet treatment. Look, I know there's hardly a decent stallion in France, but Ireland's full of them and those forty-six mares didn't go to Irish stud farms – they came here! Largely down to my friendship with Lefleur."

Charles let out a long breath. "Looking for a pay rise, are we?" He narrowed his eyes, "You're not too bad, for a Sandhurst reject."

Andrew ignored the dig. It happened regularly, and it was more an issue for Charles than him; as if it made Andrew a lesser man for not making it into the Army officer corps like Charles and his friends. He took a sip of coffee and stared out the window. The last few years seemed to have rushed by.

Andrew Dixon had grown up in the wealthy comfort of a large tract of land in Buckinghamshire, his father Jacko, a pension fund manager for a high street bank chain. Andrew had attended private schools and always had a string of ponies. His interest in horses came from his mother and her father – an old-fashioned horse dealer, master of foxhounds, and talented cross-country rider. He had been Andrew's idol as a child, and had imparted all his knowledge of horses, hounds, foxes, and life in general to the boy. His mother, Fenella, was an accomplished three-day-eventer and had competed for Britain at the Olympics in her youth.

Andrew started riding in point-to-points when he was sixteen, and after his GCSE's he became a day pupil at Stowe School, so that he could train and ride horses which he bought himself at sales. In his first season, he trained four and rode them to victory in four races each. The next year, at eighteen, he trained fifteen horses for himself, his grandfather, and friends of his parents, and ended the season with thirty-one wins. He rode them all and was crowned champion rider. People were starting to notice that Andrew Dixon was a consummate horseman.

Despite offers of work from several Lambourn trainers, Andrew said he wanted to join the Army. But after he was rejected by the Regular Commissions Board, he took a year off to travel the world, stopping off in the thoroughbred racing centres of the globe: Kentucky, Ireland, New Zealand, Australia. He returned home with his head clear, and secretly quite glad that he wasn't engaged in some rather dubious wars. He told his parents that he was going to do a two-year stint as assistant trainer to Sir Greville Thomas in Newmarket before setting himself up as a trainer on the family farm. His mother loved the idea. His father thought he should join him in the City. The thought of a life spent in London investing, juggling and hiding money, made Andrew feel ill.

2005 was Andrew's first season as a professional trainer. He trained twenty-five point-to-pointers, three steeplechasers, and one flat horse. His full height of six-foot-one forced him to give up riding after the first two months of the season. The extreme dieting left him too weak to concentrate on training. He finished the year with thirty-three point-to-point winners and two steeplechase victories. Even his flat horse managed to win once, though Andrew freely admitted that it was entirely down to the animal's ability. Those were the good old days, before disgrace tainted the family.

"Hello, is there anybody home?" barked Charles.

"Sorry," said Andrew. "I was, um…"

Charles shook his head. "No wonder you failed RCB. Right. Show Tony the stallions, convince him to replace the mares we've just sold, then I'll bring him to the house and fill him with wine and dreams. Meanwhile, you can meet Lefleur and show him the sires. I hear the Qatari Sheik provides him with a chopper. Anyway, we'll get Tony sewn up and get more mare bookings out of Lefleur. I want more than fifty out of him this year."

"Sounds like a plan," said Andrew. "Will the Earl be at lunch?"

Charles' eyes narrowed. "Jamie? No. Why?"

"It'll be purely a horse-talk lunch then?"

"Of course it will. I wouldn't want to bore the clients with his rantings about the world going to hell. Anyway, Jamie's in London for the next ten days. Oh, and I've been through my e-mails. There's rather a lot of stallion enquiries. Take care of them, will you? You know I'm not good on the computer."

That was a new excuse, thought Andrew. "Sure," he said resignedly. "Forward them on." He knew all the clients thought Charles was replying in person, but Andrew liked having access to the information. It made him feel trusted and important, even if it was double the workload.

"By the way," said Andrew, "did the police ever find out who vandalised your Range Rover?"

Charles looked momentarily dumbfounded. Then his eyes flickered. "Oh, don't worry about that, Andrew. Probably just an animal rights lunatic. They don't like that we sell stock all over the world. They think it's our duty to sell only to ethical places and buyers. Ha!" he smirked. "If we stopped to question the ethics of every owner in the horse business, we'd have a very short list of clients. You just concern yourself with running the stud."

Andrew stared at Charles, his mouth dry.

The telephone rang. Charles snapped it up. "Yes, Susan? Great, put him through... Rupert! How are you?" Charles flapped his free hand at Andrew, waving him out.

Andrew crossed the hall to his own office. He scanned through the *Racing Post* on his desk, absorbing the daily bloodstock news. The front page headline read: *Government considering offers for Tote*. Andrew grinned. He hoped Charles would be successful. Racing needed a flourishing Tote if it was to survive.

He turned his attention to the barrage of e-mails from clients, owners, and trainers.

Chapter 7

A couple of hours later, a silver Jaguar glided to a halt outside the stallion yard. Andrew put on his most winning smile and opened the passenger door, letting Lord Fowler step out into the brisk air. A poker-thin, sprightly man in his mid-sixties, he owned several breweries and had a sentimental passion for racehorses. He was immaculately dressed in tweed, like someone from another era. His striking daughter, Honor, remained in the driver's seat. Andrew grinned at her through the windscreen. She pulled a tight smile and turned her eyes to her phone.

"Good morning, your Lordship," said Andrew, beaming.

"Aah, good morning to you, Andrew," he replied, shaking Andrew's hand. "Where's Charles?"

"Still in the office, tied up on a call, I'm afraid. He'll join us in a minute."

"Haven't you been able to get him to use a mobile yet?"

Andrew laughed. "That'll never happen." He heard the clack of hooves on tarmac. "Right, your Lordship. Let's get underway, shall we?"

"Oh yes, yes."

"Good to see you, Tony," bellowed Charles, making his way across the neatly clipped lawn.

Lord Fowler turned. "Charlie! How are you?"

"Excellent, Tony. Good to see you."

The men turned their attention to the horse walking in front of them.

Charles cleared his throat and began his speech. "Ahh, here we have Capital Flight. What a horse. Won the Haydock Sprint Cup

47

as a three-year-old. Serious speed; by a good sire; the real deal. Tony, this guy's the most exciting young stallion in the country. You made a very smart decision putting your two best mares in foal to him. His first crop foals are crackers. They were well received at the weanling sales last week," said Charles.

Fowler grimaced. "Really?" He gave the stallion a good look over. "He's filled out well since last year. Looks a real man, I'll give you that. Let's hope you're right about his offspring." Fowler looked at Andrew.

Andrew opened his mouth, but the sales patter refused to spew from him. He glanced at an expectant Charles, then forced himself to nod at Fowler like a dashboard ornament.

Charles cut in. "I am Tony. I—"

"Didn't you breed him with your chum Bartholomew?" Lord Fowler interrupted. He shot a sideways glance at Charles, who pretended not to notice.

"That's right, Tony. I advised on the mating. He's out of Piers' best mare and we raced him, together with Rupert Calcott. A dream come true for all of us." He gave Lord Fowler his warmest smile.

The other six stallions were paraded, with Charles and Andrew executing well-rehearsed patter.

Afterwards, Andrew mounted his quad and led the way to the yearling barn. The others followed in the Jaguar.

Terry greeted Lord Fowler and rushed into the barn to usher out the four fillies.

Fowler grinned broadly as they were stood up in front of him. "Hello, girls, what a lovely bunch!" he said to the horses. "I'm sorry to lose you." Fowler turned to Charles, raising an eyebrow. "How much did you get for them?"

Charles cleared his throat. "Hundred and four thousand."

"Each!" Fowler beamed.

"The lot."

Fowler looked aghast, as he ran the numbers. "You told me thirty a piece."

"It's a buyer's market, Tony," said Charles. "Times are tough."

Andrew swallowed. "I'm afraid the market speaks the truth," he said. They're bad horses. That's why we couldn't find a buyer for them at the yearling sales, and they wouldn't have been good enough for the two-year-old ready-to-race Breeze Up sales in the spring."

"Where are they off to?" asked Fowler.

"Georgia," said Charles.

"Whaaat?" Fowler spluttered.

"Emerging markets are the new thing," said Charles.

Andrew agreed enthusiastically, but he wondered how much Charles'd really sold them for. The spectre of Billy appeared and made him shudder, turning his nodding into a slight shiver.

Terry sent the horses back into the barn. Fowler stood in silence, clearly fuming.

Overhead, a black and gold chopper thumped into view, skimmed the trees and made for the east lawn by the Hall.

Fowler muttered an obscenity, and looked at his watch. "What about lunch then?"

"I've a couple of bottles of Chateau Palmer breathing," said Charles.

Fowler smiled. "Now that's more like it!"

"I'll show Thierry the stallions and join you in a bit. Please excuse me, your Lordship," said Andrew, jumping on his quad. He smiled at Honor again as he drove past her. She cut him a frosty stare. Andrew chuckled to himself; he knew what Jess would make of Honor.

Chapter 8

"Thierry! Welcome."

"Andrew! 'Ow are you," said Lefleur, in his soft Parisian tones. "Good to see you again, my friend. All the mares I sent you returned home in-foal! Incredible!"

"Glad to be of service," said Andrew, shaking the ebullient man's hand. "Business must be good – arriving by chopper these days?"

"Oh no, Andrew, it belongs to Sheik Marwan Al Wahal. He likes me to use it when I'm on business. I've just come from Newmarket. I've signed up Paulie Rockford to ride for the Sheik next season, and I have to be back in Normandy this evening. Not even the tunnel is quick enough for that!"

"The champion jockey to ride exclusively for Sheik Marwan? I'm impressed," said Andrew.

"It was an offer he couldn't refuse!" Lefleur winked. "Now all we need is fresh talent in the training ranks."

Lefleur was tanned, slim, in his mid-forties, and looked like he lived on a boat on the Riviera. Andrew suspected that the smooth, refined image was all part of his slick sales act, to help him blend in with his clients and entice them to part with their money. He ran a successful bloodstock agency based in the trendy seaside resort of Deauville, and his parties there during the August yearling sales were legendary. After last year's bash, Andrew had woken up on the beach at sunrise, entwined with the daughter of one of France's wealthiest horse owners.

"Right, let's show you the new horse, then we'll talk bookings as we walk to the house for lunch. Charles is pouring Chateau

Palmer especially for you and Lord Fowler."

"Oh, you guys really know how to win a Frenchman's heart."

Royal Planet was paraded once more and Andrew began his speech.

* * *

Charles sat at the head of the long mahogany table. Lefleur and Andrew sat to his left, and Fowler and Honor to his right. Andrew held the men rapt with his assessment of last month's Breeders Cup races in America, which led into a lively discussion about the drug-enhanced state of American racing and the disdain with which other racing nations were beginning to regard US horses.

Honor couldn't take her eyes off Lefleur, though she didn't take part in the conversation. Charles' mind wandered to the money he had made from Fowler. This business just got better and better. As much as he resented the competition from the big stallion farms in Ireland, he admired the way their shrewdness had helped to change the game from a sport of kings into a business of sharks. It was the ultimate casino, where the rich clients thanked you for helping them spend their money. And if the latest batch of horses failed to win, not to worry, there were plenty more being churned out like cannon fodder.

Charles looked up at the ceiling and considered the ornate plasterwork. It would need touching up soon. More money into the pit. When he left the SAS and returned to Brockford with his wife Emma and their young son Rufus, they had moved into the east wing and Charles had thrown himself into work. A few years later, Emma surprised Charles by demanding a divorce. Few wives in her position ever abandoned ship. They usually preferred to potter about in stately homes and cold marriages, rather than venture out on their own. Charles had tried to install her in the gate lodge – vacant since his mother's death on the hunting field – so that he could see his son whenever he wanted. She'd refused and moved back to London.

Charles' features softened whenever he thought of Rufus. He was growing into a charming, polite young man, and Charles had to concede that Emma had raised him beautifully. Rufus would finish at Eton next year and would be groomed to take over the estate from the childless Jamie. At least then the old place might have a kind of renaissance – and Charles would see Rufus every day.

He feasted his eyes on the Constable landscapes and glanced at the Louis XIV commode by the wall. At least he and Jamie agreed that the furniture and art would never be sold; that was something.

Lefleur's talk of China snapped Charles out of his reverie. "I was at Sandhurst with a Chinaman, I think he's a bigwig in the Party now." Charles smirked as he remembered that fateful weekend when Ling visited Brockford.

"Really?" said Fowler. "A communist Chinaman at the academy in the 1980s? How on earth did that happen?"

"Oh, his father was a friend of their leader, Deng Xiaoping. Apparently, Deng told Thatcher to get this chap a place at Sandhurst as part of the negotiations for the Hong Kong handover agreement."

"I don't believe it!" said Fowler, astonished.

"I can assure you it's true. He even came to stay at Brockford a couple of times. Anyway, Thierry, when were you in China?" said Charles.

"Two weeks ago, for a five day tour. Racing's beginning to get going again after that setback in 2006," said Lefleur.

"What was that?" asked Fowler.

"A major investor shut down his operation. He had built a track and breeding farm near Beijing, sank millions into it, then out of the blue he pulled the plug. I suspect his political connections got cold feet."

"You say it's changing?" said Charles. "Does that mean they're in the market for horses?"

"I hope so! I think they're going to start racing on the mainland. And build a huge '*equestrian city*' near the resort town of Tianjin," said Lefleur, with a wink. "My contact told me they're sending a trade delegation on a kind of world tour in January. They want to drum up business for all sorts of things. We've been trying to do a deal with them to provide French expertise to train their people – they say it might happen eventually. But with regard to horses, I believe – just between us – they want to do a deal with the Irish for all things equine." He shrugged resignedly. "The luck of the Irish."

Charles nearly choked on his wine. Coughing, he put down his glass. "I don't bloody believe it! The canny Irish are everywhere. First, they put enormous pressure on the British breeding industry by dominating the stallion market, then they have the gall to win most of our good races, and now this!"

Lord Fowler cut in, looking at Lefleur. "At least you have the PMU betting monopoly in France to generate prize money and breeders' bonuses. What the hell have we got? Another ineffective bunch of corporate accountants who wouldn't know a horse if one bit them, trying to tell us how to run the show. Racing For Change: well they're bloody right about that. Racing for pocket change, they should call it! I love my horses as much as the next man, but I have bills to pay. I was hopeful that Catherine Fellowes could've cracked the whip and made some changes in the BHA – she was quite a loss."

Charles smiled pleasantly.

Lefleur sipped his wine and nodded sagely. "You're absolutely right." He turned to Charles. "I hear your version of the PMU: the Tote, is up for sale."

"That's right."

"Whatever happens, you can't let the government sell it to a bookmaker," said Lefleur. "Governments can make stupid decisions when they need money."

Charles grinned and shot a lightning glance at Andrew that said: *not a word*. He took a long sip of wine, savoured the taste and realised that everybody was staring at him. "Oh, er, yes," he struggled to find the words. "We won't let the government muck it up, Thierry. I'll have a chat with Eddie about it."

"Eddie?" said Lefleur.

"Edward Brookson, our Prime Minister. We were in the same house at Eton. Bloody good man. I'll discuss it with him."

"Good luck, Charlie. While you're at it, try to get the

bookmakers' powers curbed, too. More taxes and restrictions on business – that's the ticket." said Fowler. "I tried getting the House of Lords active on it, but they don't want to know. Don't have the strength for it."

Or the power, thought Charles.

"I blame the betting exchanges," said Andrew. He paused for a moment and chuckled. "It'd be nice to see the bookies chastised with tax and restricted to their dingy high street shops."

"Hear, hear," said Fowler.

"In the old-fashioned French way, we would cut their heads off," said Lefleur, sending Fowler into fits of laughter.

Andrew didn't find that funny at all. His stomach flipped as another image of Billy flashed through his mind.

Charles drained his glass. It was time to pull a few more strings.

Chapter 9

Chequers, Buckinghamshire - The following week

Rupert stood transfixed by Admiral Nelson's diary in its glass case in the Long Gallery of Chequers, the imposing Tudor mansion which had served as the country retreat of British Prime Ministers since 1921. Piers was admiring the sixteenth century tapestries and Charles was looking at some of the Cromwellian antiquities rather distastefully. They sipped brandy and waited for Eddie to finish an urgent after-dinner phone call.

Rupert took a contented swallow of the golden liquid. "Oh, that's wonderful."

"The brandy or the diary?" asked Piers.

"Both."

Charles sat by the enormous fireplace. He looked at his watch. "What the fuck is he doing?"

"On the phone with the Yanks," said Rupert. "You know how they love to talk shit."

With that, the door opened and in walked Edward Brookson, Britain's first Conservative Prime Minister in over a decade. He looked tired and pale despite his casual open-necked shirt and khaki trousers. "Sorry, chaps," he said, clapping his hands together. "Call of duty and all that. Maybe you've heard? The Chinese are sending a trade delegation on a world tour in January. Sending out their current VP, his advisors, and a team of movers and shakers. It'll be a big deal. I'll throw a reception for them here. I've just been chatting with the Americans about various arrangements."

The three ex-soldiers exchanged glances.

"We were at Sandhurst with a chap called Ling Jiao," said Piers. "I believe he's odds-on to become the next VP. Do you know if he's in the delegation?"

Eddie thought for a moment, then he cocked a finger at Piers. "There's someone by that name on the list alright, assuming it's the same guy."

"Has to be," said Piers. "They've been grooming him for this since Maggie was in power. Gosh, it would be amusing to see him again. How long will they be in town for?"

"A couple of days tops, then on to Ireland," continued Eddie, pouring himself a brandy. "OK, back to the Tote. The Chancellor has two serious offers on his desk, and I don't mind telling you that we'll probably go with Bettabet. It'll be a 200 million deal – give or take – with a cap on job losses and the guts of ninety mil going back to the taxpayer and a similar figure to racing." He sat beside Charles. "If you want me to bat for you in Downing Street, you're going to have to do better than that."

"Look here, Eddie, old boy," said Charles with a warm smile. "I will, that is, *we* will do better than that, because we *must*. I know you're not a real racing person, so I'll put it in language you can understand. We'll match their financial offer, but we won't cut a single job. We'll work on increasing turnover and put everything back into racing, so prize money gets a serious bump, and long-term, the Exchequer will have to contribute nothing to racing while still receiving a slice for the taxpayer. How's that?"

Eddie looked astounded. "Charlie, I didn't think you had that kind of liquidity. Selling off the family silver, are we?"

"That's where these two come in," said Charles, without any humour.

"And you are aware that the Tote licence goes up for grabs in seven years? That's not much time to pull off the kind of changes you're talking about."

Rupert smirked. "Well, you're only elected for five at a time, and you promise a great deal more than that."

Eddie cut him a sideways glance, which broke into a smile. All four men laughed.

"Seriously though, Eddie," said Charles. "We want to run the Tote for racing, with the express aim of funnelling off as much cash as we can into prize money. The whole shooting match depends on prize money."

"You're right, but how on earth can you do that without cutting jobs?"

"You let us worry about that," said Charles. "But I promise you, we will not shed a single job."

Eddie took a swallow of brandy and stared at a tapestry. "OK, chaps. If you get the proposal to my private secretary by Tuesday morning, I promise I'll fight your corner with the Chancellor. Anyway, it'll be an easy sell if you're not going to make anyone redundant. I'll even come out of it smelling of roses."

"That's worth a toast," said Rupert. They all clinked glasses.

"Oh and, Rupe," said Eddie. "At the moment, I don't think we have a role for your guys at the Olympics, but if something crops up, it'll head your way."

"Thanks, Eddie. I knew I could count on you."

"Not at all, Rupe. Slipstream's quite the white knight of security these days. People are wary of the Americans – too many scandals – but your guys keep their noses clean and you do so much for charity. Keeping the British end up. Good man." He raised his glass again.

Charles looked at his watch. "Well, troops, we'd better let our Prime Minister get some much needed rest."

"Oh, do stay for another," said Eddie. "It is good to catch up with all of you. Hardly ever happens any more."

"I'm sure we could manage one for the road," said Piers. "On one condition!"

"What's that?" said Eddie.

"Wangle us invites to the Chinese reception. None of us have seen Ling since Sandhurst. We really mustn't miss out on meeting him. It might be the only chance on their flying visit."

"You don't ask for much, do you, Piers!"

"Oh come on, Eddie. Surely you can pull that string for us."

Eddie looked into his brandy glass. "I can do it for you and

Charles, but I'm not sure I can risk having Rupe there – sorry. Don't get me wrong; it *could* be great for business, but if the press found out… And I don't want to have to stand on the steps of Number Ten explaining that the Slipstream boss was invited here with the Chinese VP because he was at Sandhurst with one of his aides. I'm sure you understand. You need to keep yourself low-key, Rupe."

Rupert nodded slowly. He understood alright and he did not want to make a fuss, as long as Charles and Piers got invited.

The three ex-soldiers wore satisfied grins. Phase one underway.

Chapter 10

Ling and his wife sat in the back seat of the Mercedes as it zipped out of Beijing. They were headed for their private retreat, north of the metropolis where the Kangxi grasslands stretched right up to the clear blue sky.

"I will be accompanying Guo when we make our world tour in January. We will be spending a few days in London," said Ling, a toothy grin plastered onto his face.

His wife cut him a sideways glance and a lopsided smile. "Do you think you will meet your old friends?"

Ling chuckled. "If they are still as I remember them, they will make sure that we meet during my visit."

"Then it is assured. Leopards do not change their spots."

Ling nodded.

Chapter 11

That weekend, Andrew sat behind the wheel of his treasured green Lotus Elise on a dry track at Silverstone. The tinted visor of his helmet shielded his eyes from the low winter sun as he gunned the engine. When the light turned green, he released the clutch and sped off down the straight, careful not to spin the wheels.

Andrew loved his sports car. It was his one self-indulgence, although it was spartan and budget-priced compared to most fast machines on the market. The speed and closeness to the ground was his substitute for riding a racehorse flat-out over cut birch jumps. He liked to race with the windows down and feel the air rush by. He was sensible enough not to drive like a lunatic on public roads, so he took the light, zippy machine to track days once a month and let his racing demon loose.

The faster he went, the more concentrated he became. After two laps he usually reached a zen-like state of total harmony with the car. He guided it through chicanes and round turns as if it was half a ton of rippling thoroughbred. His mind emptied of everything except the car, the track, and the drivers he overtook.

He might have achieved the same thing if he rode out for a trainer in the early mornings on the Newmarket heath, but now he could no longer race a horse, he didn't even want to sit on one.

Two hours later, he was by the parade ring at Towcester racecourse looking dapper in a dark trilby and long tweed overcoat. He loved Towcester and had won a few hunter chases here over the years. Although the stands had been renovated, they held onto their pre-war charm and gave the right-handed rectangular track a nostalgic feel, like a scene from a Snaffles painting.

Andrew sported a broad grin even as the drizzle started. Flat racing had become a corporate business, but steeplechasing was pure sport. It reminded him of the days before he spent a large amount of his time cajoling people to use Brockford stallions. The runners in the first, a novice chase, were circling in the ring, and he watched the jockeys get legged up on their muscular steeds. If flat horses were the sprinters of the equine world, these guys were the rugby players. This group of horses were still young and inexperienced by steeplechasing standards, but they had the hulking frames they needed to ply their trade in harsh winter weather. Heavy steps taken by thick limbs belied the athletic grace necessary to cover three miles and fifteen jumps at speeds nearing forty-five kilometres per hour.

The twelve runners left the paddock and cantered down to the start. Andrew marked his racecard and wandered over to the nearest Tote window. At times like this he liked to test his assessment of the runners by placing ten pounds on his pick of the paddock. He offered his note to the cashier and collected the ticket. As he turned, he bumped into a ruddy cheeked man in a battered cap and old-fashioned raincoat.

"Oh, sorry," said Andrew, tipping the brow of his hat.

"Here, you're that Dixon lad, aren't you?" said the man.

"Er, yes," said Andrew, mustering a startled smile.

"You could ride a pointer in your day! Trained a few good 'uns, too, if I remember right."

"Guilty as charged," he replied, relieved. No mention of his father or the bank.

"Here, what's going to win this? What should I stick my two 'undred on?"

"Well," Andrew hesitated. He wanted to tell the man not to waste two hundred pounds on the outcome of a horse race, and he probably would have if the man had been headed for a bookmaker. But he was in the queue for the Tote, so at least his losses would go into racing's coffers, instead of the bookmakers' satchels. "I've put a tenner on number seven, King Cookie. He looks a picture.

Trained by a good man, too."

The man looked puzzled. "That's not what the TV pundits say. Anyway, you were some man over fences in your day, so I'll take your word for it. Thanking you." He advanced to the window.

Andrew found a place on the rails, just beside a fence. He watched them approach his fence and his heart raced as they hurled themselves at it. He heard the jockeys' voices and the crackle of the fence as the horses brushed through the top few inches. He remembered how some races were like shouted conversations between the riders, punctuated with expletives as the race heated up and everybody jostled for position.

As they rounded the final bend, jockeys were silent, squeezing and flailing, driving their mounts into the last fence and up the long incline to the winning post. King Cookie was challenging the favourite for the lead. The two horses had pulled four lengths clear of the pack and were locked together as their riders urged them into the final obstacle. Andrew found himself roaring the horses up the hill, bashing his racecard off his thigh as the gallant animals plugged on to the line.

He couldn't tell which had won, so he ran all the way to the winner's enclosure behind the stands. The first three were led about in small circles by grooms as everybody waited for the photo-finish result. Steam rose into the winter air as the horses sucked in massive lungfuls of oxygen. Breaking the hushed anticipation, the judge announced King Cookie as the winner. Andrew clapped politely and was joined by many others admiring the victor.

Andrew felt his hat being whipped off his head. He turned abruptly to see Jess, her athletic frame clad in a tailored coat, pencil skirt, and knee-high boots. Her hair was scraped back into a pony tail, emphasising her cheekbones. She had a twinkle in her hazel eyes and his trilby in her hand.

"I should've known you'd stand me up for a horse. Charming," she said.

"You said *after* the first race. I thought I'd get my fix of jumping out of the way," he said with a warm smile. "Wow, you look great!"

She winked and flashed him a smile. "Thanks. I'm undercover today!"

He put his hand on her shoulder and wheeled her around.

"Come on, we'll collect my winnings. Drinks are on me."

Andrew ordered in the members' bar while Jess found two high stools near the window.

They clinked glasses. "Here's to old friends," said Andrew.

"Yeah, cheers, darlin'."

Andrew smirked, raising his eyebrows. "So, what's with the mockney accent?"

"Wha..?" She broke into a half-smile. "Well, we all have to camouflage, don't we? Do you tell your boss or those *OK-Ya* girls that your best mate's a DS in the Met?"

"D'you tell your mates you can ride and've been out fox hunting?"

"*Touché.*"

They burst out laughing.

"Where's Beatrice?" asked Jess.

"Gone."

"She find someone with money and a title?"

He sighed. "They all do in the end."

"You're after the wrong type. What happened to that French chick? What was her name? You liked her."

His face drained of colour. "Elodie. I thought she liked me, too, but apparently not enough. When her father realised it was getting serious, he forbade her to see me. Said I was beneath her. I guess she agreed with him, or she didn't want to lose her trust fund." He shrugged.

Jess punched him playfully on the arm. "Fuck 'em, Andrew. Stuck-up cows. You don't need that kind of shit."

He sighed. "Anyway, I'm off home tonight. I haven't seen my parents since September."

"You'd better hide your dad's golf clubs," she said, grinning.

Andrew chuckled.

"Seriously, though, it did look bad. How can he afford to play anyway?"

"Remember a few years ago when the club built the new driving range and the extension to the clubhouse?"

Jess shrugged. "Dunno."

"Well, he paid for it. All of it. In return, they gave him life membership including green fees, and named the bar after him. Doesn't cost him a penny to play there." He paused, smirking. "They've renamed the bar, though."

"I bet they have," Jess took a sip of her vodka. "How's your mum doing?"

Andrew let out a long breath. "OK, I suppose."

"She still drinking?"

"Oh yes, but for different reasons," he said peeling the label from his beer.

"What?"

"She used to drink to kill time between parties," he said, without looking up. "Now she does it to stay numb."

Jess looked concerned. "You should get her treatment."

"Mmm. She's a functioning alcoholic; socially acceptable. Truth is, I don't really know what to do," he stared blankly at his bottle.

They looked into each other's eyes and shared a moment of silence.

"How're your parents," he said, eventually.

"Oh, Dad's in good form. Driving Mum dotty, moaning about the state of Britain today, crime rate, etc. He wishes he was serving with me, you know!"

Andrew smiled. "He's a long time out of uniform."

"Try telling him that."

"He must be proud of you."

"Yeah." She beamed.

"When's your next bike race?"

"Next month. This is my last drink." She rattled the ice in her glass. "Hardcore training from now till victory." She leaned in towards him, still smiling. "Even if the weather's shit for the race, I'm going to kick their arses!"

Andrew could see she felt the same about cycling as he had about race riding. "I bet you will!"

She cocked her head to one side. "You still miss it? Riding, I mean."

"All the time." He glanced out the window at the runners clacking over a flight of hurdles.

"I suppose it's not quite the same being a salesman instead of a horseman," she teased.

Andrew looked shocked. "Cheeky cow! I am not a salesman. I, I–" He stopped abruptly. "Well, I suppose I am, most of the time. It's what my job seems to have turned into, without my even noticing. I love being on the farm and around horses, but…" His voice trailed off.

"You were happier when you were riding and training. Now it's like you don't have time for life any more."

"I've been pretty busy lately, I suppose."

"Lately? Ever since you started at Brockford, more like. I don't get it; what's it all for? When does it ever stop? How many horses do you need to sell?"

His eyes widened. "Well, I'm paying for Mum and Dad's house and other expenses. My wage won't cover that, so I need whatever commission Charles throws my way. I can't just stop." He finished his beer and smiled. "God, Jess, you coppers. I swear you can read my mind."

She flashed him a mischievous grin. "I was able to do that before I joined the Force."

He nodded in amused agreement. "You know, I've been thinking lately – about the horse business. Despite the crash a few years ago, it occurs to me we're still breeding too much rubbish." He explained about Capital Flight and the sales. She listened intently. "But the income keeps Brockford going and my parents with a roof over their heads."

"You could be right, too much of anything's never a good thing. I mean, there's too many people in this country, not enough jobs or money to go around, and the crime rate only goes up." She cocked a finger at him. "Look, can't you talk to your horse friends about the over-breeding thing?"

He shook his head despondently. "For all the horse people I know, they're little more than contacts or acquaintances. No real friends. If I was to mention it, they'd laugh at me. Charles would probably fire me… Or at least waterboard me into submission!" They both laughed, but the smile slipped away from Andrew's face.

"Charles'd say I'm like Catherine Fellowes. She spoke seriously a few years ago, just before the crash, about restricting stallion books through legislation; some kind of animal breed protection law. She was also on about cutting the fixture list, having a blank day each week to make life easier for trainers and staff. Everyone went mad about it. Especially the bookies. Poor woman was killed by a mugger shortly after that."

"Oh yes," said Jess. "I remember. Makes you wonder, doesn't it?" Her policeman's mind was ticking over. "With all the turmoil in the banks and what have you. Her family was famous for dodging taxes."

"She'd have been a good woman for racing."

"Her great-grandfather invented the trust fund."

"Really?"

"I'm telling you. Look it up."

"How do you know that?"

"I do read, you know."

"Not just a pretty face then?"

Jess shot him a sarcastic grin. "You should read more than the *Racing Post*."

"I do!"

They grinned at each other. She arched her brow and rattled her glass. "One for the road?"

"Alright then. What'll it be? A shot of EPO? Did you cycle here?"

"Cheeky fucker. Do I look that bedraggled?" She ran a hand over her hair.

"Not at all. You look lovely." He flashed her a smile as he got up. She almost blushed.

Andrew got the drinks and was turning away from the bar when a tall, thin, well-dressed man pushed into him. The beer fell out of his hand and shattered on the stone floor.

"Oi, steady on there," said Andrew, vaguely recognising the man.

The man was in his fifties and looked pale and haggard. He stared at Andrew with a look of pure hatred. "Wake up, cunt," he muttered, dragging his finger across his throat. "Or I'll get you and all of them."

"Now look here. What the bloody hell…"

The man turned on his heel and marched out into the crowd. Andrew rushed over to Jess. "Did you see that?"

She turned her attention away from the fifth race and gave Andrew a blank look.

"Some old guy. He knocked my drink over, called me the 'c' word, and threatened me."

Her eyes went wide. "You're joking?"

"He was–" He looked out at the people. "Nah, he's gone."

"D' you know him?"

"I've a feeling I've seen him somewhere before, but I just can't place it." He stared into space. "You know, I was accosted at the sales too, and Charles' car was vandalised." He told her all about it. "It's got to be the same guy, right?"

"Very weird," she said. A mocking smile appeared. "D'you want to fill out a report?"

"Ha, bloody ha!" They both smiled.

"Go on then, get yourself another beer."

He returned with a beer and said, "I nearly forgot. There's more. Wait till you hear this!" He told her about Billy Malone.

She listened, intent on every detail. "Bloody hell, never a dull moment in your world is there? You'd swear you worked the beat in Lambeth. Who'd you reckon did it then?"

"Everyone says he has enemies all over the place – he's ripped off half of Europe. But," he paused, screwing up his face.

"What?"

"I can't help but think it had something to do with selling Lord Fowler's fillies. The timing's a bit convenient and Charles was a bit weird about it. So was Billy, when I called him." He shrugged. "I don't know, maybe I'm just getting paranoid."

She twirled the ice in her glass. "Makes you wonder, doesn't it?"

"Racing's cleaner than it used to be, Jess, but with some of these new owners... I mean, ex-Soviet agents and Georgian billionaires. Who knows how they made their money?"

"It's not just them. That Rupert Calcott's a dodgy fucker. Private security? Huh! *Gun-toting Psychos 'r' Us*. And he's a mate of your posh boss. *Thick as thieves, my Dad'd say.*"

"I agree about Calcott, he sends a shiver up my spine, but Charles isn't all that bad underneath that army veneer. Despite what my looney assailant thinks."

She smirked. "What, so you're his mate now, are you?"

"No, but he's under a lot of pressure. Got to keep the cash rolling into Brockford."

"Pressure does strange things to people."

"Yeah, I suppose. But assault or murder?" Andrew dismissed the thought, but his stomach was doing somersaults. He found himself thinking of the photographs behind Charles' desk. The SAS weren't out in the desert on a camping trip. Rupert Calcott was probably capable of anything.

Andrew downed his beer and stared out at the racecourse.

They stayed on their stools talking until the place cleared out after the last race. Andrew racked his brains, but could not quite remember where he had seen that man before.

Chapter 12

Charles shared the backseat of Piers' Bentley. Their driver stopped at the police checkpoint and handed the invitations, identification and security passes to the officer.

The policeman tapped on the window. Piers lowered it and arched his brow at the uniformed man. The officer glanced at them and returned his eyes to the documents, while his partner ticked them off the list. The boot and the undercarriage were checked and they were ushered up the long driveway.

Chequers was alive with activity. Over one hundred and fifty had been invited to the diplomatic reception, and there were nearly as many police on duty.

Credentials were shown again at the front door and guests were given glasses of champagne and shown to the Long Gallery.

The huge room buzzed with conversation and the antiques were almost obscured by the throng. Clusters of Chinese stood around being chatted up by politicians and captains of industry, with teams of interpreters speaking rapidly.

Charles skimmed the room and caught sight of Eddie at the far end beside the Chinese Vice President, introducing those who queued up to meet the next leader of the Chinese dragon. Eddie was flanked by an aide, and to the right of the Vice President stood Ling, whispering into his ear.

Charles nudged Piers. "Target acquired."

Piers nodded. "He's aged well."

Charles smirked.

They slid through the room and joined the queue, passing their glasses to a roving waiter. Charles straightened his tie and caught Eddie's eye when they were near the Chinese delegation.

Eddie acknowledged with an almost imperceptible twitch of his mouth.

Charles almost stood to attention when he came level with Eddie.

"Good to see you. Glad you could make it," said the Prime Minister, shaking his hand. Then he turned to face the Chinese. "Vice President Guo, may I present the Honourable Charles Buckham, one of Britain's leading horsemen and an advisor to several fledgling horseracing nations. Charles, Vice President Guo Qingling."

Charles grabbed Guo by the hand and shook vigorously. Guo looked surprised, he forced an uncomfortable grin onto his face.

"It is an honour to meet you, sir," said Charles. "I have always been a great admirer of your wonderful country."

"Thank you very much," said Guo, in impeccable English, bowing from the neck.

"Last year I sold some horses to Hong Kong. What a great racing state it is! Do you plan to bring quality horseracing to the mainland in the near future?"

Guo kept smiling and cocked his head to one side, fixing his gaze on Charles. "That is a possibility, but we will have to be very careful how we handle the matter. Thank you for your interest."

"If there's anything I can ever do for you in that respect, please let me know."

"Thank you, thank you," said Guo, nodding.

Realising his time was up, Charles moved onto Ling. Piers briefly shook Guo's hand.

"Ling! My dear chap, it's been far too long! How on earth are you?" said Charles extending a hand with a sparkle in his eyes.

Ling had an immaculate navy suit covering his thin frame. His short hair was carefully parted and oiled, exactly as it had been during their Sandhurst days and his healthy complexion was that of a man ten years younger. Ling's face was a picture of astonishment. "Oh, I do not know quite what to say," he said in clipped tones, sprouting a nervous, toothy grin. "I am surprised to see you here, Charles Buckham."

"Do you remember me?" asked Piers, offering his own hand.

Ling shook it. "Indeed I do, Piers." He smiled at Piers with genuine warmth. "I remember with great fondness our late-night discussions about ancient military tactics. How are you?"

"Never better, Ling. When we heard you were coming over, we told Eddie that we just had to see you again."

"That's right," said Charles.

"Eddie?" said Ling, frowning.

"Oh, of course," said Charles. "Edward; Prime Minister Brookson. He's an old friend – I thought you'd have met him at Brockford, during your Sandhurst days?"

"No, I never did." Ling glanced over Piers' shoulder.

"Right, I can see you're busy, Ling, but I'd love to sit down and chat about the future of Chinese horseracing," said Charles, hurriedly. "What if we come out to Beijing next month? Sort of sightseeing, fact-finding mission. Could we impose ourselves on your hospitality? For old time's sake?"

Ling's eyelids flickered for an instant. "You would be more than welcome. Both of you. I will not be so busy next month and will be able to show you around personally."

"That's very kind of you," said Charles. "How should we contact you when we arrive?"

Ling produced a card from his pocket and placed it in Charles' palm. "This is my private e-mail. You can send me your itinerary, and I will arrange hotels and everything else."

"Gosh, thank you very, very much," said Charles.

"Looking forward to it already," said Piers, as they moved on and left Ling in the clutches of a high street clothing magnate.

"That was easy," Charles murmured as they weaved their way through the crowd.

"Absolutely."

"We'll bring Rupe there with us. It'll be good to get boots on the ground. If all goes well, we'll have it sewn up by summertime. One way or another."

* * *

Later that night, Guo Qingling and Ling Jiao sat in the back of their limousine, partitioned from the driver by soundproof glass.

"Who were those two men that were so pleased to see you?" asked Guo.

"I was at The Royal Military Academy Sandhurst with them. They are self-serving, though they pretend to be leaders. It is clear they want something to do with Chinese horseracing." He paused. "If Prime Minister Brookson is so friendly with them, I would question his integrity."

Guo gave his successor a sideways glance. "Do you think any world leader has complete integrity in this day and age?"

Ling smiled and flicked his eyes at the road ahead.

"You should invite them to China. Then you may learn of their intentions sooner rather than later, and on home soil," said Guo.

"Oh, they have already invited themselves. They will visit next month."

Guo grinned. "Even better."

Ling nodded in agreement and suppressed his toothy smile.

Chapter 13

Brockford Hall Stud - February 4th

A ndrew finished the last of the stallion nomination contracts. He rose from his desk, rubbed his eyes and picked up a stack of envelopes. Crossing reception, he arched his brow at Susan. "These are for posting to clients and agents, I've e-mailed the rest. Some from my own account, some from Charles'."

"Brilliant!" she grinned.

"Coffee?"

"Oh, yes please."

He returned with two cups. "I'll update the status list as they get signed and returned. Then we'll check that against the daily covering list."

"Perfect," she said with a smile. "Your system makes life so much easier. Even the most laid back of breeders know that their mares won't get covered without a signed contract."

"I should hope so, too!"

"It's just so much more civilised than all the last-minute panicking, phoning and searching."

Andrew nodded, sipped his coffee, and flicked through the news magazines on the table.

The front door opened and Charles entered, whistling. He grabbed his post from Susan's desk and mumbled, "Andrew, those magazines are just propaganda."

"Not if you read between the lines," he replied nonchalantly, without looking up.

Charles shot him a sideways glance. "You should be reading

about pedigrees, not current affairs," he said, disappearing into his office.

Andrew sighed. Charles loved pedigrees, ratings and printed facts, because he didn't really understand horses. In contrast, Andrew found pedigrees a bit boring. He was able to absorb and dissect them, but he could never understand how some people got so excited when discussing them. For Andrew, it was relatively simple: if there was enough *black-type*, you could reasonably expect a classy performer. If one knew the preferred running distances and historical details of relatives, it would help with training and development, but the real, relevant information was gleaned from observing the horse itself. That was something Charles was unable to grasp; still, it was part of the reason Andrew had a job.

Susan's phone rang. "He wants you in his office," she said, cradling the receiver.

Andrew drained his cup and made for the door.

"Gary bloody Holdsworth is complaining about our boarding fees," announced Charles. "He bent my ear for nearly fifteen minutes this morning."

"Again? We're doing the best rate we can." Andrew rolled his eyes. "I'm beginning to wonder if he's worth all the hassle."

Charles narrowed his gaze. "Don't forget, he gave you your big break with Regal Delight."

"I haven't," said Andrew, taken aback. "But he's always trying to squeeze us."

Charles cracked a smile. "I have to admit, you're right. But I want to keep him on the side a bit longer. So, knock off a couple of quid a day. Keep him happy until this Tote thing comes off, then the next time he tries it, I'll tell him we can't accommodate him and he'll either cave in or find another boarding farm."

Andrew nodded, smiling. Gary's penny-pinching would be his undoing. Andrew's grandfather's words echoed in his mind: *There are no shortcuts with horses. They've got to be tough and athletic, and that takes time, patience and money. If you can't bear the expense of doing it properly, then breed ferrets or collect stamps.*

"By the way, I'm off to Beijing on Monday, so I'll need you to hold the fort while I'm away."

"Right, no problem." He arched his brow quizzically. "Have you found a Chinese client?"

"Sort of." One-point-three billion of them, Charles thought, grinning.

Andrew looked puzzled. "Is this to do with the guy you met at Sandhurst?"

"Yes," Charles paused, drumming his fingers on the blotter. "The Tote deal looks good to go, but *not a word* to anyone," he said with hard eyes. "I don't want it leaked until the Chancellor confirms it before summer recess. If we can pull it off and give it a cash injection, it'll mean millions funnelled into the prize money pool and possibly a small bonus for all of us... If you know what I mean?"

Andrew stared.

"And that's even before we get an exclusive foothold selling our good old British bloodstock to the Chinese market.

Andrew's jaw fell open. "Chinese market? For horses?"

Charles' eyes sparkled. "Oh yes, horses. And other things."

Andrew looked at him quizzically. Charles flapped a hand at him. "All in good time. Anyway. As before, keep your mouth shut and report to me if you hear even a whiff of our Tote takeover on the grapevine. Understood?"

"Perfectly."

"Good, I'll be gone for ten days or so. Take care of my e-mails."

"What if I have to contact you?"

"I doubt you will, but I suppose I'll get you a number before we leave."

"OK then. Good luck."

"Thanks. I'm sure it'll be an easy sell, but it never hurts to have a bit of luck on your side."

Andrew wanted to ask a thousand questions, but he knew better than to interrogate Charles. The desk phone tinkled, Charles waved Andrew out and picked up.

"Hello, Charlie," said Piers in a tired voice. "I'm afraid I've got a bit of bad news. I won't make it to Beijing with you and Rupe."

"Why on earth not?"

"I'm in London, will be until the tests are over... You see, it's Julia... She fell off her horse out on the moors a few days ago. Seemed alright at first, got straight back up and rode home, but then she, well, she had these awful headaches. Silly thing wasn't wearing a helmet you see. I flew her down here last night. She's having a scan today and God knows what else. I'm quite worried, so are the girls. Poor things, they want to come out of school to visit her."

"That's simply awful. Do they have any idea what it is?"

"Not yet."

"Well, if there's anything I can do."

"Yes, of course. Thanks. I've already let Rupe know. Do have fun, and keep me posted. I have Rupe's secure number. Needless to say, you won't have a phone out there!"

"Why bother when Rupe has one?"

"What's the plan anyway?"

Charles outlined the tactics for him.

"Charlie, you're a crafty bugger. Like I said, keep me posted."

"I will if I can, but Ling arranged our hotel, so there's a fair chance we'll be monitored and escorted around like sheep."

"I'm sure you'll find a way, old boy. Bon voyage and all that."

"Thanks. Regards to the girls and fingers-crossed for Julia."

* * *

Andrew plonked himself in his chair. He was still smiling. The Tote! Charles would definitely need to increase turnover – and therefore profit – if Britain was to compete with French prize money and breeders' bonuses. And to think, Andrew would be associated with the man who pulled it off. He found his mind wandering to a utopian future where racing for massive purses kept everyone happy so they could breed athletes for racing and not fashion models for the sales ring. He even imagined Gary might stop complaining.

China. Andrew sat back in his chair. Mmmm. An exciting new

market for horses. Plenty of commission to be made, Charles was right about that.

He sighed. The smile slipped away from his face. Once again, Andrew found himself full of conflicting feelings about his job.

Billy Malone, ranting men, and tarot cards were far from his thoughts.

Chapter 14

Beijing

The black Mercedes sluiced through the toll gates on the airport expressway. Charles smiled as they zipped past the clogged lanes. He nudged Rupert. "Marvellous. Queuing's for other people. Ling's as good as his word, so far."

A stony-faced Rupert flicked his eyes towards the chauffeur. Charles took the hint and neither man spoke again until they arrived at their hotel, a shiny building towering into the sky beside the third ring road. From their suite, they had a commanding view of the heavy smog that clung to the rooftops of Beijing.

"Bloody hell, the air's filthy," said Rupert, as they attempted to survey the city below.

"They call it haze here, apparently."

"I'm sure they do," said Rupert with a chortle. "Just like we used to call opium *the balance of trade*."

Charles looked at his watch. "Time for a nap before dinner."

At eight pm they were whisked away to a narrow side street near the vast open space of Tiananmen Square. The driver opened their door and pointed to an ornate entrance. "Please, Mr. Ling is waiting for you."

Charles nodded. "Thank you."

As the two Englishmen approached, the lacquered wooden doors opened as if by magic. A bowing, dark-suited servant ushered them into a serene courtyard. There were bamboo plants growing, lanterns burning, and a fountain drizzling droplets of water from the mouth of a dragon. The servant led them through an oval opening to an inner courtyard, where a large jade statue of an ox was the centrepiece. The magnificent pavilion behind it was silhouetted against the moonlight. Charles noted the statues of guardian animals set on the apex of the roof and trailing to the turned-up corners. The pavillion doors were open and the smell of jasmine wafted into the night air. The columns supporting the structure were a rich red with gold trim, and the overhead beams were carved and painted with intricate patterns. Somewhere in the shadows, traditional Chinese music was being plucked from a lute. If there were security guards around, neither old soldier could detect them.

Ling appeared from the softly-lit interior and spoke to the servant in a polite tone. The man nodded and scurried away. Ling held out his hand. "Please, gentleman, do come inside. You are most welcome to my country."

Charles shook his hand. "Very good to see you again, Ling. This is quite a place you've got."

"That is quite a compliment, considering your palace of Brockford, but I am afraid this is not my house, as you will see."

Inside, the walls were painted imperial yellow. The room was furnished with antique chairs, low sofas and luxurious cushions. There was a round dining table with four places set.

"This was a former Imperial residence. It is now a kind of club. We use it from time to time to entertain guests. I find it more private than the usual venues."

A thin woman appeared from the adjoining room. She was dressed in tailored silk and a jade necklace, and had perfectly coiffed hair. She crossed the parquet floor with ethereal grace.

"Gentlemen," said Ling, smiling warmly. "This is my wife, Ling Xiao." He turned to her. "These are the gentlemen I was telling you about: Rupert Calcott and the Honourable Charles Buckham," he said in English.

"Good evening," she said in a perfect accent, extending a smooth hand adorned with a large diamond. "How nice to meet you."

"The pleasure is all mine, ma'am," said Charles, nodding.

"Indeed," said Rupert. "Thank you so much for your hospitality. I'm looking forward to seeing your wonderful country over the next few days."

She smiled and bowed from the neck. "Thank you."

"Please, sit down," said Ling, sweeping his hand towards the table. They took their places.

Mrs. Ling leaned towards Rupert with a twinkle in her eye. "It is good to finally meet somebody who attended your military academy with my husband. I was beginning to wonder if he was ever really there at all."

Ling laughed. "My wife has trouble picturing me in a soldier's uniform."

Rupert winked at her. "It's true, I assure you. There wasn't a man with more stamina in our year. And, if I may say so, Ling, while you may not have served in your army, it appears that life has landed you in battle, on the frontlines of politics."

"That is indeed true," said Ling.

Rupert chuckled. "If Chinese politics are anything like ours, then I'd rather be in a war zone with a gun than a parliament house trying to bend the masses to my will with rhetoric."

Ling and his wife exchanged glances.

Charles eyed Mrs. Ling up and down, as if inspecting a horse. He was less than pleased at the prospect of a night of inane small talk in the company of a cover-story wife.

"Yes, well, anyway," said Charles. "We're really looking forward to touring about. Ling, will you have time to join us at all, or are you leaving us in the capable hands of your driver?"

"I can spend a day or two with you in Beijing, but when you visit the Terracotta Warriors I'm afraid that I will not be able to accompany you."

"That's a pity, but we quite understand. So, according to the itinerary, it's the Great Wall and Ming Tombs tomorrow?"

"That is correct. It will be an early start; we will be there for sunrise."

"The Great Wall at daybreak. I bet that's a sight," said Rupert.

"It is," Ling beamed a toothy grin. "Charles Buckham, even

you will have seen nothing like it."

"Excellent!" said Charles. "Can't wait, but um, when're we going to see this new Horse City at Tianjin. I'd love to walk the track there. How's it all progressing?"

"All in good time, Charles. All in good time. Please, relax and enjoy China."

A team of waiters arrived with enough dishes of food to feed twice their number. They were placed on a revolving plinth in the centre of the table, and opened with a flourish. The delicious smells overpowered the jasmine in the air. Another servant, wearing the grape pin of a sommelier on his lapel, poured a rich, golden wine into their glasses.

"This is a Sauternes," said Ling. "I believe, in Europe, you drink it before or after the meal, but you will find it goes well with our food. I took the liberty of ordering a selection of Beijing dishes. Please, help yourselves."

Charles sipped the sweet nectar. Divine, complex flavours leaked into his taste buds. "This is sublime, Ling. Where's it from?"

"A place called Chateau D'Yquem. Several friends of mine have bought vineyards in the Bordeaux region. However, this particular chateau is not for sale. Yet."

"I didn't realise you Chinese were wine drinkers," said Rupert.

"Oh, we are learning to appreciate the delights of fermented grape juice."

"What about the delights of racehorses? Are you learning to appreciate that, too?" Charles cut in, with a hint of impatience.

"We have always appreciated that, Charles," answered Ling, in slow, measured tones. "But, personally, my interest in wine was sparked during my time in England. I also took a liking to single malt Scotch. However, I never really liked champagne. The bubbles go straight to my head."

"Indeed," said Charles, taking another sip to stifle his smirk. He remembered that weekend's leave from Sandhurst when Ling and Jamie had knocked back champagne by the pool at Brockford.

Rupert served himself food and fingered his chopsticks expertly. "So tell me," he said to Mrs. Ling. "Is it true what the international press say, that your husband is a candidate for the leadership?"

She smiled politely. "In China, it is not as simple as that." She glanced at her husband, who smiled enthusiastically. "You see, there is a leader, who is both president and – usually – Party Chief. There is also a Premier: a bit like what the French call *Premiere Ministre*," she uttered the term in a perfect French accent. "Then, there is the man your press call the Vice President: Guo Qingling. It is all but certain that he will become President upon the handover this autumn. Should that be the case, it is a real possibility that my husband will become Vice President."

Charles cracked a small grin. "Congratulations, Ling. You must be thrilled!"

Ling forced an embarrassed smile and raised his hand at Charles. "Please, please. Nothing is set in stone. It is true that Guo should be the next leader and I would be very honoured to replace him, but," he paused as if searching for his words, "it is a very delicate thing in China, passing the baton of leadership. The country must be maintained on its course with great care and harmony – we call it *weiwen* – but there are always many factions and groups who wish to steer the ship towards a course more compatible with their own interests."

"Eddie'd agree with you on that one," said Charles, chuckling.

"I'm sure he would. However, in China, we have rather more people to keep..." he frowned, looking for the right word.

"In line?" offered Rupert.

Ling gave him an expressionless stare. "I was going to say *contented*."

"Oh, yes. Right."

"Our population is large – as are our Politburo, Standing Committee, and National People's Congress – there are many things to consider and agendas to anticipate when plotting any change of course. No matter how subtle the change may appear to be, the eventual destination of the ship could be far from where it would have been. Indeed, eventually, it could even run aground."

"Yes, quite," said Charles, curtly.

"It is such a pity that Sir Piers could not come with you, I was looking forward to another discussion on tactics and politics over a bottle of whisky."

"That would've been fun for him, too. He's quite bored these days," said Rupert.

"How is his wife?" asked Ling, with a look of genuine concern.

"We haven't heard," said Rupert. "I expect he'll send word in the next day or two."

Over dinner, Charles made two further attempts to draw Ling on the subject of Chinese racing, before conceding defeat.

He would turn the screw tomorrow morning, on a wall built to keep the people in as much as the hordes out.

* * *

The car picked them up at six and slipped out of the seething metropolis. Nearly an hour later, they pulled into the car park at Badaling, a restored section of the Great Wall and one of the most visited tourist sites in the country. At this hour, the area was devoid of tour buses. Only the ticket sellers and guides were there, anticipating a brisk day's trade. Charles, Rupert and Ling stepped out of the car into the frigid air. Behind the silhouette of the wall, the first blue tones of dawn were diluting the night sky.

A hopeful tour guide approached the Westerners, until four men clad in ear pieces and outsize suits got out of a black sedan and formed a perimeter around Ling. The guide scurried towards a comrade, chattering, gesticulating, and stealing glances in the direction of the group.

Rupert ran his eyes along the wall as they walked towards the imposing stone structure. Charles looked up in awe as they passed through a heavily fortified gate tower. They walked into a paved area lined with stalls being opened by enthusiastic vendors, selling t-shirts, cheap trinkets, and caps proclaiming: *I climbed the Great Wall*. Heads turned in surprise when they saw the group. Nobody launched into a sales pitch.

Ling's guards trotted ahead up the steep steps to the battlements, scanning the vendors' faces as they went.

Standing on the wall, peering through the battlements,

Rupert let out a whistle. The wall snaked east and west to the horizon. Rupert estimated they were eight metres from the rock below and the wall was nearly six metres thick, with guard towers every 600 metres or so. As defensive structures went, it was no half measure. Even a modern invasion force would find it a challenge.

Ling let them soak it up as the sun rose into the air, bathing the scene in an orange glow.

"It is quite something, is it not?"

"I'm speechless," said Rupert. "And that doesn't happen very often. How long is it exactly?"

Ling chuckled. "It is not a simple matter of the length of one wall. There are many structures; layered, overlapping, circling; constructed over many dynasties. They total about 6,000 kilometres in length, but the main wall, which we now stand on, stretches for about 3,000 and was mostly constructed during the Ming dynasty. Of course, only certain sections have been restored to their former glory."

Rupert followed the wall to the horizon, squinting into the sun. He really was in awe. The discipline, foresight and patience it took to build this was almost beyond belief. Generations were involved and while the practical details might have changed, the grand plan remained the same. "My hat's off to you lot, Ling. This is the most incredible thing I've ever seen. During the same period in Europe, people were building walls around villages and towns, cities even. But you lot managed to fortify a country – and we're not exactly talking Andorra or the Vatican here!"

He glanced at Charles and could see he was, begrudgingly, thinking the same.

Ling acknowledged with a courteous smile and a bow. He started walking away from the sun.

"Please, enjoy the golden colours as the rays hit the stone," he said, casting his arms out wide and taking a deep breath.

Charles was biding his time, but desperate to get down to brass tacks. He was well aware that the British Empire had profited by flooding China with opium. Now he knew that their inherent compulsion for gambling would bring untold riches his way and into British racing. Different catalyst, same result.

"Ling," he started. "I really do want to discuss some business with you. I have an idea which will benefit China and Britain."

Ling smiled enigmatically. "Please, do go on."

He took a deep breath. "Right. Perhaps you already know, but British horseracing, though the envy of the world and the model for many emerging racing nations, is in financial trouble. We put on a great spectacle, but our prize money is pathetic."

Ling nodded, though Charles couldn't tell if in agreement or thought.

"The biggest problem is the bookmakers. They're like leeches, and our governing bodies appear powerless to squeeze suitable taxes out of them."

Another nod.

"So, my plan is to increase the influence and financial clout of the Tote."

Ling frowned. "Tote?"

"Oh sorry, that's our State-controlled betting pool. The profits get split between the government and racing itself. The thing is, it doesn't have the kind of power it should. So I'm in the process of buying it to stop some grubby little bookmaker snapping it up." He took a breath. "You see, I want to make it work for racing."

"And how do you plan to do that?"

"Well, that's where your amazing country would come in."

Ling looked momentarily startled, but pulled his smile back into position. Neither Charles nor Rupert missed the expression. Rupert flicked his eyes at the guards who were checking the barren ground below.

Charles continued, "I propose to broadcast one British race meeting every day in China – free to air on whatever channel you like – and split the betting profits between the Tote, you lot, and the image provider: fifty/forty/ten. Naturally, we'd have a few consultants and administrators in place over here to ensure it all flows smoothly."

Ling cut in, putting up his hand. "I will have to stop you there,

Charles. As you know, gambling is illegal in China."

Charles almost smirked. "You mean, apart from Hong Kong and Macau?"

"Yes," said Ling, without missing a beat.

"Look, Ling. Let's speak frankly."

"Oh but we are, Charles."

"Indeed." He cleared his throat. "Look, we've all heard that racing is about to get into gear on the mainland. Right?"

"That is correct: as a gentleman's sport."

"And I know that a decade ago, people said State-controlled gambling was on the way under Jiang Zemin, but the current President put the brakes on."

A nod. "Not quite that simple, but go on."

"Anyway, a great deal has changed in the last ten years. It's time to get the ball rolling. If racing is to become a popular sport, you'll need organised gambling, as you'll know from the contained success of Hong Kong. Even if you decide to race without gambling, you'll have to waste enormous resources dealing with the black market bookies. You should treat my simulcast proposal as a first step. You can keep it relatively low-key at first. You can publish the racecards in the Metro papers and open the first Tote shops in the major cities before you spread it to the countryside. With the time difference, racing'll be broadcast in the evenings so people can enjoy it after work. It'll be a winner for everyone!" he finished with his warmest smile. "What about it, old chap?"

Ling stared into the distance as he walked. An interminable minute later, he said, "You seem to have given the matter some thought."

"Indeed I have. I've even thought about the money your government'll make out of it, and how we'll be able to use our share to bolster *our* prize money and return British racing to the glory days."

Ling nodded again, with wide eyes. "As I said, you seem to have accounted for everything, but I cannot forsee the Politburo and Committee ever agreeing to such a plan. It is too radical a change of course for the country. We intend to develop horseracing here *purely* as a gentleman's pastime."

"But it's not a radical change of course at all. I mean you've already got gambling on the two islands. All you need to do is legalise it on the premises of the shops on the mainland: it's foolproof. And don't kid yourselves that your gentleman owners on the mainland won't want to gamble on their horses! Wouldn't you rather control the whole thing than tell yourselves that you can have racing without betting?" Charles was getting slightly agitated.

Ling shook his head. "I cannot see it happening." He clasped his hands behind his back as they walked.

Charles looked at the guard tower up ahead. The wall had become steep, almost a climb. He wondered if riders really used to gallop along it, relaying messages. Taking a deep breath, he plugged on. "Look here, Ling. You're well in with vice president Guo, can't you at least talk to him about it? I know you're a realist, surely you can see the good this deal would do? You chaps could use your cut for charitable purposes, just like the lottery money in Europe. Believe me, you'll make a *lot* of money out of this – surely you know how your people love to bet!"

Ling spread his arms out, palms up. "And this is the central problem, Charles."

"What do you mean?" Charles said curtly, almost at a bark. Rupert cleared his throat loudly.

"Er, sorry. What I meant was, I don't follow you. How is that a problem?"

"In this country Charles, we have one-point-three billion people. Nearly a billion of those are poor. If we introduce nationwide gambling, the middle classes will enjoy a bet, the rich, too, but it is the poor who will sell the shirt, no, the *skin* off their backs to pursue their dream of hitting the jackpot."

"You don't know that." Charles spoke in a tone that was almost derisory.

"Oh, but I can assure you I do. Furthermore, when they have done this and find themselves on the brink of starvation, they will turn their anger towards the government that permitted them to gamble."

"Well, nobody put a gun to their heads and forced them to do it."

"Maybe not, but that is entirely irrelevant." Ling stopped and took a deep breath, savouring the clean fresh air. "You see, if they got organised and found a leader, they could start a revolution."

"Which I'm sure you could put down."

Ling gave Charles a puzzled look. "If we put the entire armed forces to war against even half a billion peasants, the Army would probably be defeated after a long and bloody conflict which the world would hate us for. Nobody wants a repeat of 1989. I am sure you can still do business selling horses, services and knowledge to our rich men who wish to become racehorse owners here on the mainland."

Oh yes, a fucking pittance, thought Charles. He shot a glance at Rupert.

"Can't you help us in any way at all?" asked Rupert. "What about a sort of trial run in Beijing, Shanghai and Wuhan? Spend a year testing the waters, so to speak, before you let the masses in on it?"

Charles clenched his fist in his pocket. He considered a change of tack.

Ling nodded. "I cannot promise anything, Rupert, but it is something I will bring up tonight at dinner. Guo and I like to meet informally once a month, and that is why I will not be able to join you this evening."

Charles exhaled. He would wait till tomorrow. "That's very good of you," he said, forcing a smile. "Very good of you indeed." He clapped a hand on Ling's back, which startled him and made his guards flinch. "Gosh, sorry, didn't mean to upset the apple cart."

Ling raised his hand to the guard. "We are not used to such gestures in China." He said. "I remember your slaps on the back from Sandhurst," he chuckled. Charles and Rupert joined in.

They stopped at the tower and took in the view before returning to the cars and heading to the tombs of the Ming Emperors.

It was early evening when the car dropped them back to the hotel.

"Thanks very much, Ling," said Rupert in the lobby. "So kind of you to show us about."

"Yes, thanks,"said Charles. "And for the other thing, too."

"It was my pleasure, gentlemen," said Ling, shaking their hands warmly. "I will pick you up tomorrow morning at seven-thirty. We will enjoy the Forbidden City before the crowds arrive. After that, it is possible I will have time to escort you to Tianjin if the bullet train is running."

"Oh, that would be wonderful. You're certainly pulling out all the stops!" said Charles.

Ling smiled his toothy grin, spun on his heel and left.

Up in their hotel suite, Charles wondered if Ling would really try to bat for them with Guo. He wondered if Ling knew what was at stake and how far they would go to get it. He twirled a USB chip in his fingers. "I think Ling's going to need a bit of incentive, to help him see the big picture," he said, smiling.

Staring at the chip, Rupert grinned and cracked his knuckles.

Chapter 15

Brockford

Andrew ambled around the pregnant mares, checking their udders. Satisfied there would be no foals tonight, he climbed the fence and set off for the long field where the yearling colts resided. He marched through the crisp, sunny air and felt glad to be alive, doing what he loved.

His reverie was disturbed by a familiar chiming.

"Hi, Susan!"

"Hello, Andrew, you sound chirpy."

"It's a lovely afternoon and the horses are all healthy, what's not to be chirpy about?"

"Lord Fowler," she said in a dull tone.

"What about him?"

"He called to complain about how he faxed his mating suggestions to Mr. Buckham a week ago and hasn't heard a word. He wasn't happy that I couldn't put him through or tell him where he is."

"I did up his matings with the boss last month."

"He must've made changes. He said that if 'we' were looking for payment, we'd be all over him, but when he needs advice, he can't get a reply. Time's running out, he said. I remember putting a fax from Fowler on Mr. Buckham's desk before he left. I've had a look, but I can't see it there now."

"I'll be there in an hour."

Andrew let himself into Charles' office and installed himself behind the desk, glancing at the array of photos on the wall.

He sifted through a pile of documents held down by a paperweight that used to be an ornate door handle in a Serbian castle. No sign of Fowler's mating plans. There was a note scribbled on a torn-out page of an old sales catalogue that read: *Ling-tape-Tote-simulcast = £££*. Andrew studied it.

Next he tried the drawers; he found plenty of financial reports, lists of clients and their accounts, dozens of faxes and pedigrees of horses for sale, but no matings.

Cursing, he pulled open a bottom drawer and was confronted by stacks of junk. He flicked through old brochures, stallion books, newspaper cuttings and yet more photographs. Stuffing them all back as neatly as he could, he wondered where the list could be.

It came to him. He called Terry.

"Where are the keys to the boss's Range Rover?"

"I left 'em with Susan, soon as I got back from the airport."

"Good. Is the car at the house?"

"At the tradesmen's entrance. What d'you need it for?"

"I think he left some mating plans in it."

Terry paused. "Ooh, he did 'n' all! I saw 'em there on the back seat."

Andrew smiled, picturing Terry going through the car the moment Charles vanished into the terminal. He got up, replaced the chair, and had another look at the photo wall.

* * *

The man pulled up at the entrance to Brockford. The main gate was open. He was pretty sure he could make it to the house unchallenged: there was no electric gate until one tried to get onto the stud. The Earl apparently hated the things and refused to have one at the entrance to his own home.

Though it had been three years since he and his wife had attended a racing cocktail party here, he was sure that there was no security checkpoint either. Unusual that: a man like Charles not worried about security – except for his bloody stallions. There would be no getting near them without a pre-approved appointment. Anyway, it was wrong to take it out on the horses.

The house would have to do. For the moment.

He put the car in gear and slowly made his way up the avenue, one hand on the wheel, the other holding the fragile device.

The 11th Earl of Royston stood at the library window. Jamie's blue eyes were dull. Forlorn. The afternoons were always the hardest. Despite his longing, he still couldn't bring himself to settle down with some old dear. It was difficult enough looking at his own complexion in the mirror, without having someone heading towards ruinous old age alongside him. He much preferred the company of the young, but found it tougher to keep up with them with each year that passed. He'd had to give up bringing casual friends back to Brockford when he noticed small items of silverware had gone missing. Thieving little buggers.

He shifted a wistful glance from the Scotch decanter to the clock on the mantlepiece. Another peek at the decanter. "Must wait till teatime," he muttered. He sat on the cushioned window ledge and stared at the bookshelves. If he lived in London, he wouldn't be so lonely. Restless, he stood and made for the front door, catching his image in the hall mirror. Oh God, his roots were starting to show again. Letting out a long sigh, he returned to the library and succumbed to the decanter. He gulped down two shots in swift succession and took a third back to the window seat. The single malt hit his empty stomach like a bomb and made for his bloodstream. Jamie found himself able to smile again and let his head tip back against the pane.

A shape coming up the avenue caught his eye. He was amused to see a Bentley roll towards the house. He downed his glass, made for the front door, and opened it. An object hit him in the face and exploded. Jamie screamed in horror. A sticky liquid covered him. The car sped away in a hail of gravel as Jamie howled and rubbed his eyes.

* * *

As he had done many times before, Andrew found himself picking out the gang of three in all the photos. It was like a story of their lives, from the starched white collars and black tailcoats of Eton to the uniforms of Sandhurst and the elaborate dress regalia of the Life Guards. He couldn't quite make out the camouflaged faces in the desert, but he was sure it was them with their units. In the Sandhurst photo, his eye was drawn to the man standing beside Piers. He had noticed him before, but in light of Charles' latest trip, the man suddenly seemed more interesting. He read the name *Ling, J.* Then spun back to Charles' desk and read the note again. He stared at it, his mind whirring. No way. It couldn't be. He made for his own office to Google a few things.

His jaw hit the table when he read news reports and political opinion about Ling Jiao. If this was Charles' Chinese contact, racing's future appeared rosy indeed. He allowed himself a little smile, before he suddenly remembered Fowler's matings. He darted out, grabbed the keys from Susan and made for the house.

Andrew took the direct route out the back of the yard, through the trees, towards the avenue. His mind was still processing the potential effects of all that wonderful prize money from Charles' scheme when he heard a large car roar down the driveway. Startled by its speed, he trotted past the trees to get a look, but just glimpsed it disappearing round the bend.

Andrew tut-tutted. He hated people speeding on the avenue. Even if the stud was secure, he still had nightmares of a car colliding with a loose horse.

As he neared the old mansion, he noticed the front door was ajar, with what appeared to be red paint spattered around the frame.

Except it wasn't red paint. It was blood. Flicking open his phone, he was about to dial 999 when he saw Jamie inside. The Earl was on his knees, covered in blood, sobbing and shaking.

"Holy cow! What happened? Are you alright?"

"Oh, there you are," said Jamie.

* * *

The packed restaurant blared like a half-tuned radio. Hot and loud. That was the preferred ambience of the ordinary Chinese. The steam rising from the scalding hotpots on each table fogged the air in an imitation of the pollution outside. Diners flicked noodles from bowl to mouth and guzzled beer to soothe their palates from the spicy Szechuan food.

Guo and Ling sat at a corner table, dressed in flannel shirts. The tables around them were occupied by plainclothes agents enjoying the cuisine as much as the regular diners.

Guo sipped his beer and leaned close to his companion. "You seem to think this system is a good idea. That surprises me greatly."

"I am not necessarily for it, but having given the matter great thought on the way here, I can see the benefits. It would certainly be a blow to the illegal bookmakers."

Guo looked sceptical. "My friend, as you know, it will only inconvenience them slightly." He cleared his throat and finished his noodles. "I am open to the concept of mainland horseracing, of course – otherwise Tianjin would never be permitted," he chuckled. "They can even broadcast British racing in Hong Kong and Macau if they so wish, but never on the mainland. If we show British racing images in China, with all the prices and betting information on-screen as they do, then it will lead to massive gambling. It is a certainty. You do see that, don't you?"

Ling nodded. "Of course, of course… But, if the Tianjin facility is to be low key – hidden from the average citizen – then perhaps we could provide the service in the members' lounges there, in addition to the Wuhan venue and the island territories. It would generate considerable revenue."

Guo nodded, pursing his lips. "It certainly would, but the people working in the facility and those serving food and drinks in the lounges would spread the word. Before long they would be placing bets for their families and friends. It would not remain a rich man's secret privilege for long. Knowledge would spread and there would be an outcry, both on the streets and in the Party. Better we deny all betting on the mainland."

Ling nodded several times.

"I'm glad we agree on that. I want you to convince these men to drop the matter. However, in a gesture of fairness, I will permit them to broadcast on the islands for the proposed percentage split. Let that be the end of it. I have to visit London in June to sign a trade agreement at Whitehall, I expect I will also be required to visit their Olympic constructions and extend them great compliments on public record. I do not want to have the betting matter mentioned to me when I am there. Is that clear?"

Ling nodded. "They will be most pleased. Furthermore, I am sure their Prime Minister will show his gratitude to you."

Guo chuckled. "Perhaps."

* * *

Andrew stepped gingerly around the congealing blood and into the hall. The tarot card on the step caught his eye. He froze for an instant, staring at it: the Death card. Then he switched his gaze to Jamie. "What happened? Is this your blood?"

"No, no. At least I don't think so. I'm not in any pain. Not physically, anyway."

"Who was it?"

"I didn't see the culprit. I opened the door as this was hurled at me." Jamie picked up a fragment of a balloon. "I want the police involved," said Jamie, shaking visibly. "I know Charlie would rather take care of it privately, but not me," he said. "I will *not* have some lunatic driving in here and doing this to me or my house." He pointed towards the door but could not bring himself to look at the mess. "I need to wash, change, and have a stiff drink. Would you mind calling them and staying to support me until they leave?"

Andrew caught the scent of alcohol as Jamie made for the stairs: not gin like his mother, but whisky. He threw a sad glance at the Earl's back and hit the numbers.

The police sent a squad car from Thetford, arriving nearly an hour later, by which time Andrew had fished Lord Fowler's matings out of the Range Rover, dashed to the office, typed comments beside each proposal and dropped it with Susan for faxing.

The two bobbies took notes as Jamie described the car, but were visibly disappointed that he could neither recall the licence plate nor identify the driver. They looked at the Earl suspiciously, as if they knew he had been drinking. They seemed almost amused by the tarot card as they bagged it. One of them swabbed the blood on the door and said they would have it analysed, but the other assured Jamie it was animal blood – his brother was a butcher, he said. Definitely animal blood. This gave Jamie some relief, but the officers said that despite the expensive make of the car, without the licence number it would be difficult to track down the perpetrator.

Andrew said he hadn't even seen the car properly, let alone the driver. He considered telling them about the tarot card and the man at the sales, but an image of Billy Malone flashed through his mind. He decided to keep his mouth shut, for now.

The policemen sighed and scribbled in their notepads. Despite promising to question Charles when he got back, Andrew couldn't see it being a high priority for them. Jamie offered them tea or *something stronger*. They declined both and hastily departed.

Andrew called Terry to send somebody over with the powerhose unit and a bucket of disinfectant.

"In half an hour, it'll be like it never happened," said Andrew, cocking his head round the library door.

"Thank you, Andrew. Tell me, do you think it was somebody that Charlie robbed?" said Jamie.

"Er, no. Not that I'm aware." Andrew frowned, his mind ticking; there was something about the car.

Jamie interrupted his train of thought. "Thank you so much, dear boy. I don't know what I'd have done without you. Please, stay for tea." He knocked back another whisky.

Andrew sighed, trying not to look at the glass. "No thanks, I've got to get back." Though, having forgotten to eat lunch, he could feel his stomach rumbling.

"Nonsense," said Jamie. "I'll have Annie make up a tray of goodies. You need to eat, young man, with all the running about you do." Jamie made for the decanter. "And you deserve one of these, too."

"Definitely not. I've got too much on. Anyway, I don't like spirits," he glanced at the mantle clock. "But I will take you up on tea." He wanted to tell the Earl not to drink like this, but then if he couldn't get his own mother to listen, what hope was there?

"Excellent," Jamie drawled, with visible delight. He picked up the extension and informed his housekeeper.

Andrew ambled towards the bookshelves. "Do you mind if I browse?"

"Not at all."

Andrew selected *Anatomy of the Horse* by George Stubbs, opened it carefully on his knees, and marvelled at the ancient tome.

Jamie sprawled himself on the sofa like a teenager. "That's a first edition. Charlie professes to have read all the equine books in here, but I have my doubts," he chuckled.

Andrew ran his eye over the shelves. "Have you read many of them?"

"The Dickens' first editions are wonderful." He switched his gaze from Andrew to the Gainsborough above the fireplace. "That was the fifth Earl," he said.

Andrew looked at the painting of the bewigged man brandishing a brace of dead pheasants and a shotgun. The fifth Earl was depicted with a haunting coldness that Andrew found familiar.

"I know what *he'd* have done to somebody tossing blood on his front door," said Jamie in a sad tone. He sighed. "Bloody lunatic."

Andrew didn't know what to say.

Jamie looked at him. "I suppose the blood thrower could be someone who still holds a grudge against my stance on the environment. However, since I lost the wind farm court case, the locals tend to see me as a harmless old dear – a sort of eccentric aunty. I try to get on with them nowadays. It's nice to talk to people," he took another sip of whisky. "But it's a burden, you see. All this." He swept his arm around the room. "I love the land around it and the things we have in it, but the place itself?" he shook his head.

"But your family has lived here for hundreds of years. I thought you loved the place? Brockford's historic. It's…

well, it's worth saving, isn't it?" There was a tinge of panic in Andrew's voice. He and Charles worked so hard to keep the place running. He couldn't believe his ears.

Jamie shrugged. "It's an anachronism. It consumes too many resources. Should we destroy ourselves trying to save it? Or should we move on to a more sustainable way of life? I tried to do it my way, but nobody's ready to listen to an ageing poof preaching to them about the environment. It seems that Charlie's business – oohh, now *there's* a dirty word," he shuddered, "is the only way to save the place, but I find myself wondering if that's a price I want to pay."

Andrew realised he was staring slack-jawed at the Earl.

Jamie's blue eyes bored into the younger man the way Charles' sometimes did. "Charlie's positively Cromwellian, you know. He's obsessed. He'd do anything to keep Brockford private. He hates the idea that strangers would pay to look around, and frankly, so do I. I'd rather sell." Another sip. "You know, my father used to say that businessmen were nothing but tatty rogues, but perhaps if *he'd* been a *bit* of a rogue, then Charlie wouldn't need to be such a shit. That's what he is really, underneath the smile and polish." He drained the glass and refilled it. "We had a sort of relationship before he became a soldier, but the Army brought out the worst in him." He wagged a finger at Andrew. "You should be careful. He's accustomed to getting what he wants, by whatever means necessary."

Andrew closed the book. He was about to speak when a smiling Annie appeared with tea and sandwiches. Jamie put his finger to his lips. Andrew thanked the sprightly widow and tucked in. Jamie pecked at a sandwich like a small bird, but his eyes looked ravenous.

"Does Charles know how you feel?" said Andrew.

"We argue about it almost daily. I'd rather live in London with all the paintings and art around me. I want to sell the house and gardens. Charles could keep the forestry and stud, build himself a house on it and we'd have plenty of cash to go around, but he won't hear of it." He paused, giving Andrew a lopsided smile. "And you're not helping much, Mr. Gung-ho stud manager."

"Me? I thought we were fighting the good fight. Keeping the wolf from the door sort-of-thing."

Jamie burst into a deep, guttural laugh. "*Dear* boy, do wake up!"

Andrew was bewildered.

"Stop drinking Charlie's *kool-aid*. The wolf isn't at the door; he lives in the east wing."

* * *

Ling and his wife lay in bed. He pored over his laptop while she read.

He snapped his device shut and rolled towards her. "Buckham has shown his hand." He told her about Charles' proposal.

She arched her brow and dropped her book. "And how did Guo react when you discussed it with him?"

"As expected."

She gave her husband a thin smile and a peck on the cheek. Then turned out the light.

Chapter 16

Beijing

Charles, Ling and Rupert were on the battlement of Meridian Gate, the main entrance to the Forbidden City. An elaborate pavilion stood atop the structure and from their vantage point, they could see past Tiananmen Gate, with its massive picture of Chairman Mao, to the vast expanse of Tiananmen Square stretching into the smog. Below them, throngs of cyclists battled for space with cars on Chang'an Avenue. It was a symphony of chiming bells, punctuated by shrill voices and car horns, everything underscored by the simmering drone of engines. Beijing on its way to work.

All three men wore heavy overcoats, and steamy breath rose from their mouths. Ling had instructed his guards to remain in the courtyard below. They blocked access to the stairway and prevented Palace Museum officials or visitors from disturbing him. High up on the battlement, he wanted complete privacy to deliver his message.

"I have some very good news regarding your racing matter," said Ling, without averting his eyes from the traffic.

Charles stared at him impatiently, rubbing his hands together.

Ling shot him a sideways glance. "Vice President Guo has agreed that you may broadcast your racing in Hong Kong and Macau, with wagering, and for the proposed percentage split."

Rupert looked at Ling with wide eyes.

"What about the mainland?" said Charles.

"He cannot agree to that. It will never happen in his lifetime. It is just too dangerous for the country."

Charles closed his fist around the USB stick in his pocket. He could possibly support Brockford with whatever they made from Hong Kong, but with Rupert and Piers to be paid, there would be little left over for racing's coffers. Without a visible increase in prize money, the house of cards would soon collapse. That was unacceptable. He took a deep breath. "I'm afraid that won't do at all, Ling. You see, we need more exposure than that. The major cities on the mainland have to be part of the deal."

Ling shook his head. "Gentlemen, you will make plenty of money with the proposed arrangement, and the ship will not deviate from its course. You simply must accept this, or take your offer to Japan or Korea."

Charles flicked a glance at Rupert. Calcott ambled nonchantly towards the stairway. Charles brought his fist out of his pocket, clasped it with his other hand, and spoke in a slow, thunderous murmur. "Now look here, Ling. If you think I'm going to waste my time setting all this up for bloody pocket change out of Hong Kong and Macau, you are seriously mistaken," he said. "I haven't bought the Tote as a fucking plaything. I *need* your gambling rights to make it all work, and by Christ, I'm going to get them. You must accept this."

Ling looked slightly amused by the sudden outburst.

"You'll get the deal done. Understand? I don't care how many strings you have to pull, bribes you have to make, or dicks you have to suck. Just get it done. And don't give me any more bullshit about revolutions. *Money talks*, and if you and your cronies are making enough of it, the plight of the peasants will be irrelevant. Ling, I know how rich your Congress members are. They love money as much as the next man. Don't forget, there are *billions* at stake here."

Ling's cheeks were glowing red, but his tone remained calm. "You come to my country, accept my hospitality, and talk to me like this? I understand your business needs and respect our history together, that is why I did you the courtesy of arranging the islands' deal. But now you step over the line, Charles Buckham. As I suspected, you are just another greedy colonialist. This is not the nineteenth century, we Chinese do not have to play your games anymore. You must play ours. Go home, Charles. We have nothing further to discuss." He turned to walk away.

Rupert blocked the stairs, arms folded, teeth clenched. As Ling opened his mouth to shout, Charles darted a fist into his stomach, doubling him over. Charles quickly grabbed Ling by the collar, pulling him upright. Ling's face was a crimson mask of horror. Charles opened his fist, revealing the small black USB chip. He pushed it into Ling's mouth. "Go somewhere private and watch this. It's you and my brother having sex by the pool at Brockford. Rather nostalgic, don't you think?"

Instantly, the colour drained from Ling's face and his muscles relaxed. He spat the chip into his hand as if it was poison.

"That's much better, old chap. I can see I've finally got your attention." Charles wore a sinister grin. Delight danced in his eyes, making them brighten to a cobalt shade. He saw something flash across Ling's features. Could've been fear.

Ling spoke calmly. "Charles Buckham, you have made a serious mistake. I will have you arrested, you will not leave this country until I give the word."

Charles kept grinning. "By all means arrest us. Throw us in jail if you feel you have to. But if I were you, I'd have a look at that chip before you do anything rash." His steely eyes cut into Ling. "And remember," he jabbed a finger at Ling's chest, "that's only a copy. I can have it all over the internet in an hour and the British newspapers within twelve. Oh, and I can assure you, the result will be the same if anything should happen to Rupe or I out here. So calm down, trot back to your office, and give the matter some thought. Rupe and I'll go to Tianjin on the bullet train as planned. We only need one of your goons to tag along and interpret. Be a good chap and tell the others to piss off."

Ling opened his mouth. Hesitated. Snapped it shut. Straightened his coat.

Rupert moved from the stairway. "It's probably best if we leave as we arrived," he said, with a sly grin.

They made their way back to the cars in silence. Ling dispatched them to the train station with a guard before stepping into his own Mercedes.

* * *

They had first class seats on the bullet train. Charles relaxed, grinning broadly. He cast his mind back to 1985 and the day they discovered Ling and his brother locked together in passion. It was instinct that told him to keep the camera rolling, but it was Rupert's inspired idea to retreat in silence and keep the evidence a secret. Until now. He wished he'd taken a photo of Ling's face today: priceless. Ling hadn't expected that.

The suburban sprawl flashed past in a blur and before they knew it, Charles and Rupert were in a taxi headed for Tianjin Equine Culture City.

They were dropped at a huge, tiled entrance gate. Their minder barked at a foreman and moments later, a double-cab jeep was produced. The minder ushered them inside, but the ex-soldiers hopped up on the flatbed. They pulled on gloves, flicked their collars up, grabbed the rail. "Drive on!" roared Charles with a haughty grin.

They were driven about the 900 acre site. The oval racetrack looked nearly finished, Charles estimated it at 2,000 metres round. It was completely covered in plastic to protect the new grass shoots from the harsh Beijing winter. The foundations were being laid for a grandstand of gargantuan proportions.

"Looks like they want to outdo Dubai," said Rupert. "I read there's going to be a seven star hotel here."

"And they think they can have all this without gambling? Either they're desperately naive, or they plan to cut off a few heads as a deterrent." Charles shook his head. "Even then, they'd never prevent it."

They passed a development of Western-style villas and into a newly completed polo club where Rupert thought he saw a foreigner leading a horse into a cathedral-like stable barn. The three grass pitches looked as smooth as a snooker table, and there were two indoor arenas for winter play. They drove on, through a new plantation of mature trees – a manufactured forest built around a maze of riding trails and cross-country fences. The trees gave way to the bones of what would become another luxurious stable complex and show jumping stadium. Four all-weather olympic dressage arenas were next. The jeep slowed to let them admire a series of proud billboards showing computer mock-ups of an equine science university, feed factory, veterinary hospital and a rehabilitation complex, complete with swimming pools, treadmills and hyperbaric chambers.

They passed through another row of trees and came to a halt. In front of them, neatly railed paddocks were arranged in almost mathematical fashion. There were five long stable barns in various stages of construction and what looked like a stallion yard, breeding shed, and office complex.

Charles rubbed his hands together. "This'll all be ours, Rupe. We'll unload our failed stallions – starting with Capital sodding Flight – and many more things they don't yet realise they need."

Rupert stared at three men standing by a half finished stable barn. One was clearly a Westerner; he was drawing in the sand with a stick and talking to the locals, who responded with toothy grins similar to Ling's standard expression. "Let's have a word with that guy." He thumped the roof and the jeep stopped. The ex-soldiers hopped off the back and marched towards the men.

Their minder hurried after them. "Please, please. What you do? No time! No time!"

They ignored him.

The Westerner saw them approaching. He put down his stick, pinched the bridge of his nose, and spoke to the locals. "OK, lads, that's enough for today. Sorry, but you'll have to tell the builders to re-do it in the morning. Thanks, lads." They scurried off, chattering wildly.

He stuck out his hand. "Well, lads! Nick Brennan, how's it going? Jesus, it's good to see a Western face." Nick's eyes were sunken and encircled by black rings, but he shook their hands firmly.

"Charles Buckham."

"Rupert Calcott."

"What brings you lads out here?"

"A bit of reconnaissance," said Rupert. "Are you part of the Irish mission?"

"I am indeed. Been here six weeks, tryin' to get the farm sorted before the first lot of horses arrive," he shook his head. "Place is a shambles. They've all the kit and no end of money, but not a clue how to get it done. Bunch of engineers thinking they're horsemen." He raised his hands. "Don't get me wrong now, they're lovely people and bursting with enthusiasm, but they've a lot to learn."

Charles laughed. "They're tough little buggers to get to the bottom of. Keep cracking the whip and you won't go wrong."

Nick frowned. "You think? Not really my style. Besides, I've noticed that they clam up and stop altogether if you lose the plot."

"Not at all! Spare the rod, spoil the child," said Charles, thrusting a business card into the Irishman's palm. "Look, if you ever need any help, or even just someone to talk to, give me a shout any time."

"Thanks," he said, reading the card.

"Well, we'd love to stay and bring you out to dinner, but our plane leaves this evening. Very good to meet you."

They all shook hands again and parted company, much to the relief of their minder.

"He won't last long," said Rupert, mounting the jeep.

"I agree, he looks half-frazzled already. With Ling's help, we'll get them to see the light, cancel their deal with the Irish, and come running to us."

* * *

Back in the hotel that evening, Charles was changing for dinner. Rupert appeared from the adjoining room with a gin and tonic.

"Not much taste out of this," he said, sinking into a chair.

There was a knock at the door. The two men exchanged gloating smiles.

Charles opened the door on a stony-faced Ling.

"Been watching home movies?" said Charles, shutting the door behind Ling. His guards remained outside, blocking the corridor.

Ling cleared his throat. He remained calm. "Firstly, you have got it all wrong. Despite what you have caught on camera, I am not *gay*."

Charles couldn't tell if he uttered the word in a tone of embarrassment or disgust. "Hmm. Now look here, Ling," he began, wearing a pleasant, thoughtful expression. "It might be difficult for your Committee, and indeed your population, to understand your point of view when they see, all over the internet and the world's media, my brother *giving you a fucking blow job!*" His cheerful tone gave way to a thunderous roar.

Ling jumped, startled. "I–I, was a drunken young man, taken advantage of by your brother."

Rupert let out a chortle. Charles wagged a finger. "You've got me there. Jamie always loved to try it on with anyone new. However, once I publish the footage and it's verified as you – which it will be, you've hardly changed at all – nobody'll give a shit about the details. You'll be disgraced and your career will be over." He clicked his fingers. "Just like that." He cocked his head to one side, feigning a puzzled look. "Do they still shoot gays here?"

Ling opened his mouth as if to speak. Charles cut him off. "Or do they just expect you to commit suicide?"

Ling stared at the wall for a moment. "Charles Buckham, I'll see what I can do. I will consult with the more liberal factions in the National People's Congress at the forthcoming annual meeting, starting March fifth. It will also be a suitable opportunity to test the waters in the Standing Committee. I will suggest gambling centres on the facilities in Tianjin and Wuhan along with other centres in certain rich suburbs of Beijing, Shanghai and Guangzhou. Will that be satisfactory?"

"I suppose it'll do for a start." Charles had to concentrate to suppress an ecstatic smile.

"However, you must assure me one thing. When Guo Qingling makes his visit to London in June, nobody will mention a word of this to him. It would be catastrophic for me – for all of us. I will find a way forward, but it must be found and structured before he learns of it, because he is the principle obstacle that we must manoeuvre around."

Charles narrowed his eyes. "Guo's coming to England again?"

"Yes, for a trade agreement in mid-June."

Charles shot a glance at Rupert, who narrowed his steely eyes. "I will expect to hear from you before then," said Charles.

Ling nodded rapidly three times, his smile wider and toothier than usual. Rupert thought he noticed a glint in the man's eye.

Charles grabbed the door handle. "I'm so glad we got that sorted. We're off to Xi'an tomorrow, then home the day after. If any bizarre accident should befall us here or in England, the footage will be published. Oh, and then Rupe's men'll hunt you down and do simply awful things to you. Is that clear?" They shot Ling their coldest gazes. Rupert cracked his knuckles. Ling dashed through the open door.

Charles felt like dancing a jig. Phase two underway.

"Reckon he'll come through?" asked Rupert, mixing two more drinks.

"I'm bloody sure of it. Fear and leverage, old chap. Fear and leverage." Charles moved to the window and sipped his drink, "You're right, no flavour. Anyway, if he starts dithering about, we'll get to work on Guo during his London visit…" He stopped, lost in thought. After a moment, he snapped his fingers. "Mid-June! Bloody marvellous! We'll get Guo to Ascot for a day, treat him like a sodding emperor. Soften him up with a bit of British pomp, show him what a regal, classy occasion racing – with gambling – can be."

"Bloody good idea. No harm to open up another front on the attack." Rupert's nod turned into a frown. "What if he won't accept the invitation?"

"Mmmm. I suppose we could always collar him in Whitehall, but it wouldn't be the same." He sipped his drink and thought for a minute. "Don't worry, he'll accept the Ascot invitation because it'll come from Buckingham Palace. Nobody turns down an invitation from the British Royal Household. They're the world's number one celebrities. I'll get Eddie to bring it up at one of his weekly sessions with Her Majesty."

Rupert mulled it over for a second and his features brightened. "That's positively inspired, Charlie. Stroke of genius! Eddie'll go for it, too; it's the perfect way to cater to Guo's ego, it'll grease all kinds of wheels."

"And at the very least, it'll get him deep into our turf. One way or another, we'll have it sewn up by August."

Rupert pulled out his smartphone. "I'd better e-mail Piers and put him out of his misery. He's been trying to call me all day. I don't see why the fuck he couldn't come."

"Just because I'm divorced and you don't love your wife, don't assume that it's same for everybody," Charles snapped. "Sometimes, I envy Piers," he muttered. His thoughts turned to Rufus; he hadn't seen him in so long. When he returned, he would take the boy out of Eton and treat him to Sunday lunch.

* * *

Piers sat in the plush armchair, staring at his wife as she slept. The scan at the Harley Street Clinic had revealed a hairline crack in her skull and the doctors had recommended that she stay under observation for a few days. Piers refused to leave her bedside until she was given the all clear. He had sent a car to bring his daughters from school for an hour this afternoon, which cheered them all up.

His iPad pinged. He read Rupert's message three times, a giddy grin plastered on his red face. "Proper job, men," he muttered, then frowned as a brief wave of sadness passed over him. Poor old Ling; stuck between a rock and a hard place. He was not the first politician to get caught having inappropriate sex, nor would he be the last. Piers shrugged. "Can't be helped, old chap. That's life," he muttered, as he tapped out a reply.

* * *

They stood on the gantry overlooking the Terracotta Army. Visitors walked the circumference of the three excavated pits, gazing down over the 8,000 warriors that had taken thirty-six years and a conscripted workforce of 700,000 to complete. Charles and Rupert admired the scene in reverential silence.

Rupert's smartphone pinged. His breath hissed through his teeth.

"What?" said Charles.

"It's from Piers: Subject: *Horse flied lice*." He rolled his eyes and read the mail aloud.

"How's his wife?" asked Charles.

"Doesn't say. Christ, he's like a kid with his iPad: sent me a juvenile joke, too. Oh, look, he cc'd everything to you. Now that's a waste of fucking time! Anyway, what do you reckon?" asked Rupert.

"I think he's on the right track," said Charles. He continued in hushed tones, flicking his eyes about as they walked. Rupert lapped up the details, feeling his heart quicken. "It'll almost be like the old days," he said.

"Only far more profitable."

Both ex-soldiers felt the buzz of adrenaline; heightened awareness, sharpened perception. They quickened their pace and grinned in anticipation of a satisfying victory. They took one last look at the ancient army before leaving the museum.

Charles clapped his hands together. To the victor the spoils.

Chapter 17

Andrew barely slept that night. He could not get Jamie's words out of his head. Billy Malone's accident was definitely connected to the Fowler deal, and if Jamie was to be believed, Charles was probably capable of beating him up personally. It was sickening to confront the idea that Charles was guilty of assault just to get a few horses sold, and disheartening to realise he hadn't a clue what to do about it. As for the man at the sales, well.... Andrew thought about calling Jess, but he knew she would ask him if he had proof. His mind flashed back to the morning the news had broken about his father: he hadn't wanted to believe that either.

The alarm beeped and he dragged himself out of bed and checked every horse on the farm without uttering a word. Then he waited for the vet to arrive. An hour later, he went to the stallion barn and looked at Capital Flight in his stable. It was Valentine's Day; the stallions would begin covering tomorrow.

Charles, like almost every other stallion master, had always insisted that coverings began on February first, and had encouraged many breeders to "get a head start on the season" by breeding before the traditional start. However, a couple of years ago a Monaco-based businessman had paid a seven-figure sum at the Newmarket December sales for a pregnant mare covered on February seventh by an Irish-based sire. Nobody told the mare that she must carry her foal for the full eleven months. She decided to give birth ten days early, on December twenty-seventh. Her owner was appalled that his new foal would officially turn one year old just four days after its birth. The Jockey Club and the BHA refused to grant

110

an exception and the owner sold all his horses and quit racing in protest. Most stud farms went into panic mode and returned to the February fifteenth start. Except for a few, who continued to tempt commercial breeders to roll the dice. Andrew felt it would be silly to risk it, and Charles reluctantly agreed.

In the office, he found Susan and Terry jabbering eagerly about yesterday's action. Andrew smiled. They would probably give the matter more consideration than the local Constabulary.

"Morning, all. Are we good to go for tomorrow, Terry?"

"That we are," he said with a wink. "The boys are mad for sex!"

Susan rolled her eyes. "I've had nine bookings already, Andrew."

"Excellent. Are the contracts rolling back to us?"

"Steadily."

"Good. So, back to your gossip. What's the verdict on the blood-thrower?" said Andrew, leaning on the desk.

"I'm damned if I know," said Terry. "It's a strange business and it's not like we've a list of angry clients who'd throw blood at us."

"Well, I think it's disgusting," said Susan.

"You should've seen the mess on the front door," said Terry, winking.

Susan turned up her nose and went back to her work.

"Funny thing is," said Andrew, "I was abused at the sales and the races back in December. Charles' car was vandalised with blood there, too. Come to think of it, he never did much about that."

"You what?" said Terry.

Susan stopped typing and looked over her glasses at Andrew.

"Some guy accosted me in the bar, called me…" He hesitated to use the word in front of Susan. "Called me the 'c' word and walked off."

"He never!" said Terry. "Why didn't you say anything?"

"I did, to a friend of mine – she's a detective in the Met. We just kind of shrugged it off. Thing is, I think I recognised him."

"It weren't the same guy yesterday, was it? I mean blood on the Range Rover and now the house!"

Andrew shrugged. "Seems likely, but I don't know for sure.

Didn't see him. Only heard the car zooming down the avenue. Jamie, er, The Earl, said it was a green Bentley."

Susan's eyes were wide. "That's rather a posh car for a vandal."

Terry arched his brow. "Poor old Mrs. Fellowes had one o'them, may she rest in peace... Don't suppose it was her come back from the dead?" He chuckled.

Susan cut him a disapproving stare.

Andrew stared at Terry. His mind was... It hadn't occurred to him yesterday, but he'd seen a green Bentley somewhere else recently and... No, no. It, it...

"You look like you've seen a ghost," said Susan.

Andrew half-heard her through the fog of muddled thoughts. "What? Yes, no. Look, I've just remembered something about some, er, contracts. Got to check them on the boss's PC..." His voice trailed off as he made for Charles' office and shut the door.

Shooting a contemptuous glance at the photo wall, he sat at the desk and pondered. The hum of the cooling fan reached his ears and he realised he had left the computer on. He tapped the mouse, bringing the device out of sleep and glanced at the list of e-mails.

Two new ones from Piers: one smutty joke with a clip of some jiggling breasts, and another entitled *Horse flied lice*. Andrew rolled his eyes at the feeble attempt at humour and was about to shut down the machine, when he became curious for a bit of inside information on China. He opened the mail and read it: "*Chaps. Thanks for the news. I say, if the little poofter can't get it done, instead of the pool footage, why not give it the Anatolian shove? Sort of pave the way, kind of thing?*"

Even by the childish standard of Pier's bigoted jokes, this was truly bizarre. He shook his head, closed the inbox and clicked *shut down*.

Then he emptied the bottom drawer onto the desk. He began going through the clutter again, putting everything back in its place as he went.

He got to the old folder and flicked through the cuttings. There it was. His heart skipped a beat. The front page of the *Racing Post*.

He read the headline about the BHA Chairman's shocking, tragic death. There was a quote from the BHA Chief Executive: "*We are all struggling to come to terms with the sudden and tragic loss of such a dynamic and likeable woman.*" *Jockey Club Steward Sir Piers Bartholemew was quoted: "Further terrible proof of the despicable criminal element lurking in the underbelly of the wonderful racing town of Newmarket.*" Prepared soundbites, if ever he read them.

And there it was, under the text and in full colour: a photo of the crime scene. Police officers milled around a body covered with plastic, lying beside a blood-splattered Bentley. The next photo made Andrew gasp: *Mr. and Mrs. George Fellowes attending Royal Ascot in 2010,* said the caption. It was him, no doubt about it. Sure, he was dressed differently and had lost a few pounds since the photo, but the man who had accosted him at the races was definitely George Fellowes. Must've been him at the sales, too. Andrew sucked air through his teeth and rubbed his chin. It had to have been him yesterday, it just had to. Green Bentley. Tarot card.

Andrew slumped at the desk and buried his head in his hands. What had Charles done to make Fellowes so mad? Billy Malone crept into his head again. Murder? Ridiculous. Catherine Fellowes wasn't a trainer-come-agent, she didn't even board mares at Brockford and, to Andrew's knowledge, had never even patronised the stallions.

The desk phone cut the air with a shrill ring. Andrew jumped. Reluctantly, he picked up.

"What the fuck are you doing in my office?" barked Charles.

Andrew threw his eyes about. Were there cameras in here? Relax, he told himself. Don't get paranoid: Susan put the call through. He cleared his throat. "I'm going over Lord Fowler's matings again."

"Oh, right. OK."

"Um, did the Earl tell you what happened yesterday?" he said, hastily changing the subject.

"No. What are you talking about?"

"Oh, well it's probably best he tells you."

"For God's sake, spit it out."

Andrew immediately regretted bringing it up, but if he hadn't, that might have made Charles suspicious in the long run. He swallowed hard. "Well, basically, somebody pulled up to the house in the afternoon and threw a balloon full of blood at the door."

There was silence for a moment. Then, "Do you know who it was?"

"Er, no, no. No idea. I didn't see him. Neither did the Earl; he only saw the car. The police don't seem too bothered about it."

"The police? Oh, fucking hell. Look, I'll deal with it all when I get back. Can you tell Terry to pick me up tomorrow evening?"

"Sure, no problem."

"How's everything on the farm?"

"Great. Sires start covering tomorrow and mares're foaling without a problem. Um, how did your trip go?"

"Oh, very good. I've done a deal to simulcast British racing in China with Tote betting."

"Sorry, did I hear you correctly?"

"Yes, you did. My connection's setting it all up. It'll bring millions into racing's coffers."

My connection. An image on a grainy photo popped into Andrew's head. "Er, that's marvellous!" he blurted.

"Not a word to anyone, Dixon."

"Of course."

"I'll tell you the rest when I get back. Any gossip on the airwaves?"

"Not a thing. Come to think of it, I don't think anyone knows you're in China."

"Good." The line went dead.

Andrew hung up and realised his heart was pounding. As he put the cuttings back in the folder, his eye was drawn to a small article on a page dominated by the November Open race meeting at Cheltenham. The Turkish Jockey Club president had been killed in a hit and run outside a busy Istanbul restaurant.

Andrew remembered that Charles had brokered the sale of six British stallions to the Turks that year, just before Christmas. He recalled the frantic rush to get all the paperwork done and the horses out of quarantine and onto the plane before the year ended. Andrew had been relieved to see the stallions leave the English gene pool, not a decent sire among them in his opinion. He'd never understood how Charles got fifteen million for them. Surely not?

Then again, it had taken him a month to accept that his father had really said and done all those things, even after the evidence was paraded all over the national newspapers.

Andrew stumbled back to his own office in a blur, vaguely aware of Susan trying to tell him something. Flopping into his chair, he called Jess. Voicemail. He couldn't bring himself to leave a message. He would call her tonight.

He sat there shaking his head, reminded of the day the news had broken about his father. Jacko Dixon was caught trying to leave his bailed-out bank with a golden parachute of ten million pounds, yet he still couldn't account for the lost pension funds. A disgruntled secretary had leaked the story to the press, along with mobile phone footage revealing how the cavalier banker conspired with the board to take "his" money and slip away quietly. He could be heard saying: "*Fuck the people, they were queuing up to invest and now they have the gall to complain that it didn't pay off.*" In the fallout from the scandal, the bank had to sack him and press charges to save face. He'd escaped jail, but the courts seized his estate and forced him to make a public apology. Andrew had barely believed it, even when he had seen the footage on a TV show.

Jacko Dixon now spent his days in denial: golfing and anticipating a return to the world of high finance.

Maybe Andrew had been drawn to Charles as some kind of surrogate father-figure, similar in so many ways to his own.

Andrew's stomach was spinning like a washing machine. He sighed. It would be nice to get drunk and blot it out for a few hours, but that was probably what his mother thought every afternoon, and it never really solved anything for her.

Instead, he pulled a Directory of the Turf off the bookshelf, and looked up a number. His hands shook with fear as he searched.

Chapter 18

Whip and Spurs Public House, Stetchworth, Suffolk

That afternoon, Andrew pulled his cap down and slipped into the corner booth. Through the window he watched the road, waiting for the green Bentley to pull in. His palms and armpits were clammy and the second hand on his watch seemed to operate in slow motion. It was five past four and the place was deserted, except for a pickled-looking man slumped at the bar, boring the landlord with bitter rantings about when he told so-and-so how to train such-and-such to win the Derby. Of course, the trainer didn't take his advice and the horse didn't win. Bloody fools, the lot of them.

Andrew whipped his gaze to the door as the hinges creaked. George Fellowes greeted the landlord with a forced smile, ordered a gin and tonic, and folded his lanky frame into the seat opposite Andrew. He pulled off his battered trilby and tossed it on the table.

Even in the poor light of the old pub, Andrew could see the man was gaunt and his nose and cheeks were near purple and mapped with veins. He stared at Andrew with barely concealed anger.

"You requested the meeting. What do you want?" he spat.

Andrew shrugged in an effort to appear relaxed. "I'm not really sure." He stared at Fellowes. "What's your problem with Charles and me?"

"Pah," Fellowes waved his hand dismissively. "Don't play dumb. You wouldn't have called me if you didn't already suspect.

Unless *he* put you up to it?"

"*He's* not even in the country. If he was, there's no way I'd have agreed to meet this close to home. Tell me what you know – or think – and I'll tell you what I suspect. Fair enough?"

"Quite simply, I believe that your boss killed my wife."

Andrew stared, his mouth open.

"Oh, I don't imagine for a second he did it himself. Probably got a Slipstream savage to do it while he was having dinner somewhere public, but he was behind it."

"Why would he do that?"

Fellowes cocked his head to one side like an animal regarding a strange object. "Think about it."

"I've done little else the past few hours. Your wife was appalled by the excessive overproduction in the thoroughbred racehorse. She saw it as damaging to the breed and made noises about restricting stallion bookings, but – no offence – people laughed at her. Nobody took her seriously." He paused, looking downcast. "Even if she was right. Because even now, after the market crash, we're still covering too many mares."

Fellowes sat up, surprised. "That's a change of heart by the Brockford boy."

"Yeah well, long story. Anyway, that's not the point. Why would Charles kill somebody that nobody was listening to, even if he disagreed with her politics?"

"What you don't know was that Catherine *was* taken seriously by a growing number of people. She had nearly every small breeder in the Thoroughbred Breeders' Association on her side, and she had an animal welfare group poised to put pressure on Westminster. Catherine argued that the American Standardbred gene pool had been destroyed by the use of artificial insemination coupled with unrestricted mare numbers for their stallions, and that the thoroughbred would be weakened by similar reckless overproduction, even if AI remained illegal. She was on the cusp of a breakthrough before…" His voice lost steam and Andrew saw his eyes moisten. He took a long pull on his gin.

"I know that pompous git Bartholomew got wind of her plans,

because I heard him blowing about it in the Jockey Club Rooms one evening. He's another Buckham crony."

"Yes, but—"

"Oh, come on, Dixon. You know how fanatical Charles is about Brockford. Your whole business model depends on large books of mares for your sires. If Catherine had succeeded, you'd have had to shut up shop."

Andrew chewed his lip, then he nodded, conceding the point. "Correct. But so might a lot of other farms."

"No other farm that I can think of is controlled by someone like Charles Buckham," he leaned in close to Andrew. "What do you know about Charles' army days?"

"Not a lot really. Life Guards, SAS. The first Iraq war, Serbia. That's it; no details. You know, from time to time, I have wondered exactly what he got up to."

"I don't know many details either, but I do know this: my brother served alongside him in The Regiment."

"The SAS?"

"Yes. There was an incident in the Kuwaiti desert, during the invasion."

"Go on."

"Piers Bartholomew might be the richest, and Rupert Calcott the meanest, but Charles is the real commander. He outranked the others in The Regiment. He covered up the Kuwait incident for his pal Calcott. The details are sketchy, but supposedly Calcott's unit ended up at the wrong RV point, two SAS men were killed, dozens of innocent Iraqis were murdered, and their village burnt to the ground to cover it all up. During the inquiry, Charles said his unit received a distress call and arrived to find their comrades under heavy fire, they joined the fight and that was that," he took another drink. "The thing is: word got around that that wasn't what happened at all – soldiers gossip amongst themselves like everyone else – but Charles silenced those directly involved. It wasn't too difficult really. The brass were only too happy to buy the tidy story and avoid tarnishing The Regiment's heroic image."

"Holy shit!"

"Indeed. So you see, Buckham and Calcott got a taste for it back then: murder without consequence. And now they have far more power than you can possibly imagine."

Andrew looked quizzically at the wretched face in front of him.

"They have our Prime Minister's ear. Eddie Brookson went to Eton with them. And Calcott, through Slipstream and its subsidiaries, has a finger in every pie and a private army to do his bidding."

"What about Piers?"

"Huh, I know on the outside he seems like a bit of a jolly hockey sticks type, and he's certainly more humane than the other two – at least he used to be – but he's a shrewd tactician. He's very good at keeping himself out of harm's way; rumour has it his NCOs nicknamed him *Teflon*." He paused. "Charles is the boss. He's a dangerous man, Dixon. Watch him. Watch yourself."

"Why don't you go to the police with all this?"

"Haven't you been listening? *Me*, go up against *them*? I can't prove a thing. The police'd dismiss me as a paranoid, grief stricken old fool who watches too many films. I did approach a local journalist, but he virtually told me to seek psychiatric help. Huh! Anyway, I don't really… That is to say, I'm not really… Not since Catherine died. You, on the other hand…" His voice trailed off.

Andrew decided not to press the man further. "OK, so here's what I suspect: I'm sure that Charles had a guy beaten up just to get a better percentage on the sale of four yearlings."

"Who?"

"Billy Malone – Irish guy. Trainer, agent, general moneygrubber."

"Oh yes, I remember that. Little devil had enemies everywhere."

"That's what everyone says, but I'm sure it was Charles." Andrew recounted the whole episode to Fellowes. "Also, I think he had the Turkish Jockey Club president done in so he could get a bunch of useless sires sold to Turkey."

"Nothing would surprise me."

Andrew felt strange, he rubbed his temples. "That brings the suspected body count to two. Plus all those Kuwaitis, and God knows how many guys he's beaten up…"

His head started to spin, and he dashed to the toilet as vomit gushed into his mouth. It was not a pleasant thought: assistant to a murderer. Andrew wondered if Jamie knew. Was that why he drank? More blotting out of reality?

He rinsed himself and returned to the table. "Sorry about that. I, I…" He shrugged, lost for words.

Fellowes almost smiled. "Now you know how I feel every day. All that knowledge and no bloody proof."

Andrew cleared his mind. It was time for action. "I've a friend who's a DS in the Met. I'll go and have a chat with her, figure out a way to get him – them. There has to be something we can do. But please, George, no more blood balloons. Just lie low and take it one day at a time."

Fellowes scoffed. "So you're giving the orders now, are you?"

Andrew frowned. "No, but your version of deranged grief isn't going to get us anywhere."

Fellowes nodded begrudgingly and put his hat on.

Andrew continued, "I'll have to go back to work as if nothing's wrong, keep doing my job, and see what happens."

Fellowes stood and turned to leave, then he stuck out a hand. Andrew shook it. "Thank you for listening and believing," said the widower.

"You're welcome. Oh, by the way, what's with the tarot cards?"

"My daughter was into them when she was a teenager. I thought they might get you thinking."

"Maybe it worked."

Andrew heard the large engine growl as the Bentley pulled away. He downed his Coke and walked out. His head down and mind full, he almost bumped into a man locking his car right outside the door. He rounded the corner, got into his Lotus, and took the Newmarket road.

* * *

John Smith was locking his old Ford when he felt someone brush his shoulder and hustle past. Looking up, he called, "Oi, watch where you're going!" and thought there was something familiar about the younger man disappearing round the corner.

Moments later, he saw a green Lotus zip onto the road, headed for Newmarket. He tut-tutted, shaking his head. "You'll end up in a ditch at that rate, Dixon."

He ordered a pint of his favourite ale and phoned his brother Terry to give him all the latest gossip.

Chapter 19

That night six mares foaled. Terry never got to bed so he left word for Andrew that he would sleep until the afternoon.

At seven am, the breeding season started with a bang. All eight stallions covered mares and the farm bustled with lorries and trailers. Andrew supervised the matings, greeted breeders and lorry drivers who brought their mares, and showed them the refreshments in the waiting room. Afterwards, he dashed to the office to check contracts and phone clients.

Next, he checked the newborn foals and did his usual rounds of the farm. He felt like a military officer directing manoeuvres, and was so busy that he pushed all thoughts of Charles' deeds to the back of his mind. The thrill of running a busy stud farm like a well-oiled machine filled his brain with satisfaction, as it did every breeding season.

When he returned to his farm cottage for a quick sandwich, he read a newspaper article announcing a forthcoming trade agreement between Britain and China. The spectre of Charles reappeared.

Andrew rubbed his temples and made plans. Terry had to pick up Charles that evening, but he'd be back in time to attend to any foalings. So Andrew called Jess and arranged to pop down to London. He couldn't help but smile when he heard her voice.

They sat on her sofa with the pizza box between them. Jess crossed her athletic legs underneath her and sat enthralled as Andrew recounted the events of the last two days.

"Bloody hell," she said. "That's some story, but you've got no evidence. Nothing. What do you want to do about it?"

He shrugged. "I was hoping your copper's brain might help me."

She nibbled on a slice of pizza, lost in thought.

He looked at his watch. "Charles should be back by now. Oh, that reminds me, I'm beginning to doubt his intentions with this whole Tote-China deal."

"You what?"

"Oops! Charles swore me to secrecy," he said, smirking. He told her what Charles had said on the phone. "Lately, I don't believe Charles'd do anything for the common good. If he's telling me that he's buying the Tote to put more money in racing's coffers, then it's probably just a cover story. More likely he's doing it to line his own pockets. Oh yeah, and he's got a high-ranking Chinese official in his pocket."

"How d'you know that?"

He told her about Ling.

"You sure about all this?"

"Well, I don't think it's coincidence."

Jess looked doubtful. "I don't know, Andrew. Do you think the Chinese'll ever allow gambling on the mainland?"

He sucked air between his teeth. "People've been waiting for that to happen for decades, but Charles was confident. So I guess Ling's making it happen."

"Hang on, you're telling me that your boss is buddies with our PM and the next Chinese VP?"

"Seems like it."

"OK, assuming for a second that it's all true. Then, like I said, what do you want to do about it? The Turkish thing's a no-go; even if you had evidence, it's not our jurisdiction. True, the Fellowes case is still unsolved, but I can't imagine any detective's going to want to dig it out again unless there's a serious lead. And again, all you have is a theory. Come on, Andrew, even if he gave the order, it'd be impossible to pin it on him unless you got the goon that did it, and even then…"

"I know Jess, really I do, but I can't let it go." He rubbed his face in his hands. "Would you let it go if you thought you worked for a murderer?"

"Fair point."

"Hey, maybe I should get him on tape, like that secretary did to Dad?" He shot her a lopsided grin.

She looked sceptical, arching her brow. "I didn't hear you say that."

Their eyes met and held for a moment. Andrew opened his mouth as if to speak, then he broke away and got two more beers from the kitchen. Jess followed him with her eyes.

"That's your third," she said, taking hers as he plonked himself down. "Looks like you're staying here tonight."

He took a swig. "Yeah, you're right. Safer that way. Do you mind?"

"God, no. I'd be pissed off if you drove after three beers."

"And I wouldn't want to incur your wrath!" he said, giving her a sideways smirk.

She had a twinkle in her eye. "No, you bloody wouldn't. Cheeky sod!" She flicked the bottle top at him, catching him on the forehead.

He returned service with a chunk of pizza crust. She caught it and began munching, "Cheers, mate." She winked.

They held each other's gaze for a second. Andrew broke the silence. "Hey, those earrings are new. They look lovely on you…" He narrowed his eyes. "Who got you those?"

"What? Oh, er, thanks. Yeah, they're nice, aren't they?" she said, fondling the pearl adorning her lobe. "I treated myself after winning that race."

"They're classy. They suit you."

She blushed and chewed her lip. Andrew looked as if he was about to speak, but he took a sip of beer instead. She stood and began tidying up. "I'm done with this beer, do you want to finish it?"

"Er, um, no thanks."

"I'll get you a duvet and pillow," she said.

Returning, she offered him a toothbrush as well.

"Thanks, Jess,"

"G'night." She gave him a peck on the cheek and disappeared

into her room as he prepared his bed.

The next morning she went to wake him and saw the neatly folded duvet sitting on the empty sofa. A note on the coffee table read: *Thanks, Jess. You're the best. Belated happy Valentines Day! There's fresh coffee waiting for you in the pot. Call you later.*

She smiled. It was a start.

* * *

Terry pulled out of the snarling mess of the M25 and sped away from London. He loved driving the Range Rover. It was a clear evening and the SUV ironed the roads as smooth as a duck pond. Though he was weaving through cars doing nearly eighty, it felt like they were barely out of a trot in the leather and walnut-trimmed interior.

Finally on the open road, Terry could contain himself no longer. He launched into a torrent of gossip about everything that had happened while Charles had been away, saving the best till last.

"That blood-throwing vandal must've been old George Fellowes. Hell of a mess 'e made." He let the remark hang in the air.

Charles whipped his cold eyes to Terry. "What on earth are you talking about?"

"Reckon Andrew must've figured it out, too, and gone to have it out with 'im. John saw old Fellowes leave the Whip and Spurs yesterday in his sodding great car and Andrew stormed out afterwards and sped off like he was in a Grand Prix."

"Is this fact, or more of your embellished gossip?"

"As true as I sit here beside you. John'd recognise that Lotus of his anywhere, same goes for Mrs. Fellowes' old Bentley. He may drive a bit fast, but he's a good 'un that Dixon. Done more about it than the coppers ever will. I expect he told Fellowes where to stick his vandalism. Don't worry, Fellowes won't bother us again, I'd say. Andrew has a friend in the Met, too, that'll keep old Fellowes at bay, don't you think? Thing is, I can't figure out for the life of me why he'd want to do it at all." He glanced at Charles and hastily put his eyes back on the road. Maybe he had said too much.

Charles' face was a picture of dark thunder. He curled his hands into fists and shot his gaze out the window. His synapses fired like machine guns. That was a bit close for comfort. Still, what could Fellowes really tell Andrew? Probably nothing without ranting and raving like a lunatic. But Andrew was in my office, and if he saw Piers' e-mail? What else did he know? And why meet Fellowes, why not tell the police? Who was his friend in the Met?

Charles took a deep breath and stared at the passing countryside.

Still, one should not be rash. The breeding season was underway and Andrew was good at running the farm, chasing up contracts, seducing clients and judging foals. For the next five months, he'd be too busy to think about George Fellowes and his ranting and raving. However, it could be useful to set a trap.

Chapter 20

Andrew started the day as usual; coverings, rounds of the farm, checking horses. Afterwards, he found himself doing mundane jobs in an effort to avoid the office and Charles. He put down the pitchfork and sighed. He couldn't postpone it any longer.

Not for the first time that morning, Jess crept into his thoughts. He tried calling her. Voicemail again. He left a stuttering message, and cursed himself for sounding like a teenager.

Outside the barn, Andrew swung a leg over his quad and pressed the ignition. Terry came trotting out of the tack room. "Ere he is, our own detective!" he said with a chortle.

Andrew was lost for words. Startled, he could only manage a confused look.

Terry winked. "I know you went and kicked old Fellowes' arse for 'im."

Andrew went pale. His mouth was dry.

Terry stared at him in mock surprise. "Oh, right you be. Mum's the word." He tapped his nose. "Say no more."

Andrew cleared his throat and finally spoke. "Terry, what are you on about?"

"You sound like Charles. C'mon," he scoffed, "John seen you leaving the pub the other day. Said you had a face like a bag of hammers an' all."

Andrew's mind was reeling. "You told Charles that?"

"Course I did! So," he glanced about and leaned towards Andrew, "you give 'im a proper dressing down? Did he tell you why he did it? 'Cause I've got to say, I'm buggered if I know."

127

Andrew did his best impression of Charles' icy glare. "Look, Terry. Please, for once in your life, stop shooting your mouth off about things that don't concern you. If I'd wanted you to know, I'd have told you. OK?"

"Alright, alright. Don't get your knickers in a knot."

Andrew gunned the motor and set off for the office, his stomach doing somersaults.

"Oh, there you are," said Susan. "Mr. Buckham wants to see you." She rolled her eyes towards the door and mouthed, "In a foul mood."

Andrew didn't know whether to feel resigned or terrified, and probably looked both. He gritted his teeth and entered the lair.

Charles looked up from the documents on his desk. "Ah, there you are. I've been going over the mare numbers," he said, smiling. "Slightly up on last year, which is wonderful considering the British foal crop is still in decline. Well done!"

"Er, um, thanks." He pulled his face into a smile that did not reach his eyes. "Well, it's partly due to all the continental mares. Thierry came through with nearly sixty this year."

"He'll be counting his commission already, no doubt. Still, good work, Andrew." He kept his eyes fixed on his manager. "Of course, we're not up with Irish numbers yet, but it's a start."

Charles' cordiality wrongfooted Andrew. "Yeah, great. Good," he said, sitting down. He scanned the desk and noticed a DVD in a clear plastic cover amongst the papers. It was unmarked, apart from an L scrawled on it. He averted his eyes and saw Charles scrutinising him.

"So," said Charles. "I wanted to let you know that I expect the Tote deal to be done the week of Ascot. Has anyone been talking about it?"

Andrew shook his head. "Not a word, as far as I know." He took a deep breath. "So you've really secured simulcast rights in China? With Tote betting?"

A flicker of anger rippled across Charles' face before he could mask it. "Yes, yes, of course. We've got a few details to iron out, but it's basically done."

"That's brilliant! British racing'll be in your debt – quite literally!"

Charles frowned. "Hmm. Indeed."

"So, they'll open up gambling then?"

"Oh yes, they certainly will. It'll be restricted to the major cities at first, but once the Princelings realise how much money they'll make, it'll spread like cancer." He cracked a sly grin. "Our cut of the revenue will be massive."

Andrew whistled. "British prize money'll go through the roof."

"Indeed. But more importantly, Brockford, your job, and your nice cash bonus, will be safe for the foreseeable future. That's wonderful news, don't you think?"

"Absolutely," he said, nodding hastily.

"Again, not a word until it's signed and sealed."

Andrew nodded. Charles picked up the foaling list. "I see we've had five Capital Flights hit the ground. Any good ones?"

Andrew winced. "The birthweights tell the whole story, I'm afraid. Rabbits, the lot of them."

"Yes well, can't be helped. One can't make silk purses, et cetera. I think we'll be able to unload him on the Chinese. They've a farm almost ready to go in Tianjin; just the place for a Brockford cast-off."

Andrew was surprised and curious. "That's great, but I thought they were dealing with the Irish for all that?"

"Oh, I think I'll be able to shove the Irish out the side door."

"Seriously? That's great news. How'll you manage that?"

"What the Chinese call *guanxi*. Contacts. It's the way it all works out there."

"Great. What's the Tianjin farm like?"

"Apparently, they've made a bit of a pigs ear of it, but we'll let the Irish deal with that. Once it's up and running, I'll send you out there to have a look. You can meet our contact and go through whatever bloodstock they already have. Then we'll tell them what they need to buy from us."

"I'll get a trip to Beijing?"

He smiled warmly and cocked a finger at Andrew. "If you play your cards right."

"Brilliant. Thank you very much." Andrew flicked an eye at the Sandhurst photo. "What's your Chinese contact's name anyway? He must be well-in there?" He couldn't help himself but ask.

The smile vanished from Charles' face. "We'll get to all that later. Now, you must tell me all about your meeting with that mad old coot Fellowes. How on earth did you know he was the blood-thrower?"

Andrew could feel his body temperature rise, his palms were suddenly clammy. He cleared his throat. "Oh, well, I was with His Lordship when he told the police about the car and I remembered seeing Fellowes getting out of it at Towcester races one day last year. Initially, I thought I was putting two and two together and getting five until I called him and he started shouting and abusing me. So, I insisted we meet and he suggested the Whip and Spurs."

Charles sat back and twirled his pen. "Really? Well done, you, detective. Did you find out why he did it?"

Andrew's eyes flickered as he processed options. "No. I, er, I asked him alright, but he just got angry and called me and you cunts. So I warned him that if he ever came near the place again, I'd make a full report to the police. That seemed to quieten him down. Then I left."

"You what?"

"I left the pub."

"And you didn't grill him on why he did it?"

"Like I said, I asked him, but he wasn't making much sense. Kept calling you a bastard. He wasn't exactly rational." He shrugged. "I just supposed he'd had business with you that went sour." Andrew hoped he was convincing enough.

"Did you now?" The stare was intense and frosty.

"Well, yes. Look, I know he's never sent a mare here, but you both have horses in training with Mark Saville. Maybe he's just jealous?"

"Jealous? Ah yes, the green-eyed monster." Charles tossed the pen onto the desk. "That must be it, because for the life of me, I can't figure it out either. Anyway, forget about the old fool and tell me about this friend you have in the Met."

Andrew's heart skipped a beat. His mind whirred. He remembered mentioning something about it in front of Terry and Susan. Had he mentioned Jess by name? He didn't know. Bloody Terry.

"We've known each other for ages."

"Since when did you hang around with coppers?"

"We grew up together."

"Did you now? What's this friend's name?"

Shit. He would have to tell him. "Jess."

"Jess what?"

"Jess Flint."

"She's a close friend, is she?" he said, winking.

"No, not like that. In fact, we don't see each other that much anymore. Our lives are drifting apart." He didn't really believe it as he said it, but he was worried that it might be a little bit true.

"Huh! You look smitten."

"What? Er no, she's just a friend." But he blushed a deep red. He stood and looked at his watch. "I'd better get cracking, lots to do. Was that all?"

"Yes, yes. You get on. We'll go through the foals after lunch. Meet me at barn one, will you?"

Andrew nodded and left. Back in his own office, he slumped in the chair, took a deep breath, and replayed the conversation in his mind. What was Charles planning? Andrew concluded that he needed to have another root around in his office.

When the door closed, Charles swivelled his chair and looked at the Sandhurst photo. He turned back to the desk and opened the bottom drawer. He reached to grab the old stallion brochures, but his hand stopped in mid-air. The cuttings folder was not usually on top of everything. He swore and picked up the DVD on his desk. He was about to lock it in the filing cabinet, when he had an idea. He picked up the phone.

"Hello, Rupe. Is this line secure?"

"Of course. What is it?"

"George fucking Fellowes. The old fool can't let go or deal with his grief. He's starting to raise eyebrows."

"Oh dear. That won't do at all."

"No. I'm going to need a few bits of kit from you."

"Certainly. Fire away, whatever you need. I'll have Goran drop them down to you."

A week later, a white Mercedes van pulled up at the Hall. Charles answered the front door and accepted the small package. "Thank you, Goran," he said.

The swarthy, besuited man nodded. Goran moved like a panther as he crossed the gravel and slid into his seat.

Charles shut the door and spun on his heel, cradling the box.

Behind him, Jamie was on the stairs, leaning against the bannister. "Who was that, Charlie?"

Charles pulled a smile onto his face. "Oh, stud affairs. Nothing you need to worry about," he said, as he made for the east wing.

In his private sitting room, he opened the sealed package and smiled. Just the job; he would have a practice session, then wait for the right opportunity.

Chapter 21

Deep inside the vast concrete structure, Guo Qingling sat with two aides in the Beijing Meeting Hall. It was a small room, perfect for intimate gatherings and in sharp contrast to the enormous auditoriums which dominated the building.

Guo needed respite from the endless networking, bargaining and speeches of the annual *Liang Hui* – the twin meetings of the National People's Congress and the People's Political Consultative Conference, that took place in the Great Hall.

He had ordered the room sealed off to allow him time to prepare for the evening's keynote addresses that would bring the ten-day event to a close. He finished reading the final draft of his speech, sipped jasmine tea, and fished an envelope from the diplomatic pouch on the table beside him.

The invitation was written on crisp, thick paper, headed with the emblem of the British Royal Household. He read the printed text twice and closely inspected the signature. After a minute, Guo dismissed his aides with instructions to fetch Ling Jiao, then he sat back and stared at the gigantic porcelain vase in the corner.

Soon afterwards, Ling walked in and sat beside him.

Guo tossed the invitation onto Ling's lap. "Please," he said with a smile.

Ling nodded sagely as he read the text. This was a most interesting development. Ling stifled a smile. "A personal invitation from Her Majesty The Queen. This is a very great honour and a definite indication of how highly the British value trade with China."

Guo shrugged. "Perhaps. But I am assuming this is because of your friends, and not necessarily the idea of their government or monarch."

Ling nodded reluctantly. "It is a distinct possibility."

Guo leaned close and put his hand on Ling's arm. "I told you what I would allow. If they find that unsatisfactory, then that is their problem. Furthermore, I cannot be seen attending an event at which gambling is a central activity."

"My *friends*," Ling looked ill as he uttered the word, "know how you feel and the matter is, shall we say, closed. But *this*," he tapped the notepaper, "is nonetheless an invitation from one head of state to another who will shortly assume office. Politically, it would be a great insult to refuse. But if you attend, it will put the British in the palm of your hand." He paused, smiling. "You know, I attended that race meeting once, during my year at their military college. It is nothing like Hong Kong. It is…" He stared at the silk screen by the wall, searching for the right words. "It is a bit like Disneyland for the aristocracy and their horses. For them, it is a celebration of horses, royalty, social uniforms, and the pomp and ceremony that they are so famous for. I assure you, it will be a most interesting day."

Guo pursed his lips and sat in silence for a minute. Then he barked into the phone by his chair. Moments later an aide silently appeared at his side. Guo dished out his orders rapidly. The aide scribbled frantically on a pad and nodded like a dashboard ornament.

Ling wore a pensive frown. Guo's visits to the London Olympic venue and Royal Ascot should provide ample exposure and publicity.

* * *

Charles was fed up. He knew the big Chinese pow-wow had ended five days ago, and he was not inclined to believe that no news was good news. Ling had not bothered to call, and his e-mails had gone unanswered. To top it all off, nobody had informed him whether Guo Qing-fucking-Chong had replied to the Ascot invitation.

He screwed up a sheet of paper and hurled it at the bin. Then he dialled Eddie's mobile. Turned off. What was the point of having a mobile phone if it was hardly ever on? He yanked open the top drawer and found the Downing Street numbers.

"Good afternoon, the Prime Minister's office," said the secretary in clipped BBC English.

"Good afternoon. This is the Honourable Charles Buckham speaking. I wonder if it's possible to have a quick word with the Prime Minister."

"I'll just see, sir. What is it regarding?"

"It's a personal matter," he snapped. "Just tell Eddie who's on the line, please."

A pause. "Certainly, sir."

He tapped his pen off the blotter as he was kept on hold. Eventually, the secretary came back on the line. "I'm sorry for the wait, sir, the Prime Minister will be with you momentarily."

"Thank you." He kept tapping for another five minutes, until a familiar voice addressed him.

"Charlie! How are you? Sorry about the wait. It's all go around here, as you can imagine."

"Oh, I can, I can, and I won't keep you. I just wondered if you'd heard anything from the Chinese about the Ascot thing."

"Oh yes, that's all good to go. The Queen's private secretary contacted my office yesterday. VP Guo has accepted. He'll attend the first day of the meeting and he'll have a seat in a carriage for the royal procession."

Charles smiled into the receiver. "That's wonderful news, Eddie."

"I think it's a great coup, too. He was already scheduled to have a discreet lunch at the Palace with Prince Freddie and a few ministers, but Ascot's the icing on the cake. Bloody good idea of yours, Charlie."

"My pleasure, Eddie."

"Of course, Her Majesty isn't too sure what to make of it, but she's putting duty first, bless her. The only drawback is we'll have to rush him through the Olympic Village that morning, but I suppose that's not the end of the world."

"No. Anyway, I take it our Tote thing is on target for the summer?"

"As a matter of fact, it's slated for the week before Ascot, so you'll have something to celebrate when you welcome Guo to the races. I have to say, Charlie, your plan is audacious, but if you pull it off, you'll be quite the white knight of racing."

Charles grinned and punched the air. "Oh, you know me, Eddie, just trying to do my bit."

"Yes, quite. As long as that's all it is, Charlie."

"Of course, old boy. Of course."

"Charlie, there's a lot riding on the trade agreement. You wouldn't do anything to muck up the big picture, would you?"

"Eddie, I'm shocked you'd even ask. I'm a big picture sort of chap. Always have been. As I said, I just want to show Guo how dignified and classy a race meeting – with gambling – can be, and make him understand the benefits of doing business with us."

"Good. Right, got to run. Chat later."

The line went dead.

Charles sat back and rubbed his hands together as he pondered the next step. It was time. Dickie Phipps was coming to lunch tomorrow; that would provide the perfect excuse. He unlocked the filing cabinet.

The next day, while the staff were on their lunch break, Andrew was helping the vet administer plasma to a newborn foal. Halfway through the procedure, his pocked vibrated: Charles.

"I'm having lunch with Dickie Phipps in the house, could you pop into my office and get me his matings list?"

"The one we did last night?"

"That's the one. I thought I had it with me. Bring it here. If you hurry, you'll be in time for pudding."

"I'm stuck with this foal till everyone gets back from lunch."

"Oh, alright. You'll miss the apple crumble though." He hung up.

Andrew looked at his watch and called Colin. "Can you get to the foaling unit in five mins? I've to do something for the boss."

Colin said he was on his way.

After nearly a month of nervous waiting, this would be Andrew's first, and perhaps only, chance to look through Charles' desk again.

Andrew hustled past Susan, muttering something about Dickie Phipps, and shut the door behind him. He sat at the desk, found the matings list and left it ready to snatch if anyone disturbed him.

Then he tapped the mouse and brought the screen out of sleep mode. He accessed the inbox, read Piers' *horse flied lice* e-mail several times and decided to print it off. There was a sent message to Ling Jiao politely asking for a progress report. He printed that, too. What next? He opened the top drawer and flicked open Charles' address book. He scanned through it hastily, but there were no details or numbers for anyone in China. There was nothing under F for Fellowes, but there was a number for Yildiz, Okan. It had been crossed out.

Andrew was about to close the drawer, when he flipped to the Bs and looked at the array of numbers under Brookson, Eddie. Many had been crossed out as new ones were added. Only three appeared to be current. He jotted them down.

Next, he opened the bottom drawer and saw the DVD sitting on top of the pile, a red L the only identifying mark. He removed it from the cover and opened the disc tray on the computer. Then he thought better of it, closed the drawer, grabbed his illicit bundle and dashed across the hall. To his relief, Susan had stepped out for her post-sandwich walk.

His own computer seemed to take an age to boot up. When it was ready, he inserted the disc. There was only one file on it. His finger hit play and his jaw hit the desk.

It was the swimming pool he recognised first. Though Charles had made Jamie close it down two years ago, citing expense and lack of use, Andrew recalled enjoying it during his first summer at Brockford.

The image was slightly grainy and obviously re-formatted from VHS, but the two men were clearly visible as the camera zoomed in. Jamie. It was definitely a young Jamie and… And… Holy shit!

He opened a web browser and compared the photos he found of Ling Jiao to the image on-screen. The man had hardly changed in thirty years.

So that was how you got the Chinese to open up mainland gambling. It all began to make sense.

Still unsure exactly what he should do, he rifled his desk, found an old USB chip and plugged it in. He hit *send to* on the disc menu and the file began to copy. He drummed his fingers on the desk as he watched the progress line stutter through the small percentages.

His phone chimed, making him jump.

"Coming, coming. I have the list," he blurted.

"Don't bother. Stay at the office. I'm on my way down with Dickie," said Charles.

Sweat poured off Andrew. "Come on, for fuck's sake, come on," he muttered at the screen.

Then he heard the outside door open. Panic gripped him. He stood, popped the tray, stuffed the disc into his windcheater, and burst into reception.

He found himself staring stupidly at Susan.

"You look like you've seen a ghost," she said, taking off her coat.

"Me? Er, no. Just doing matings. The boss is on his way here with Dickie Phipps."

"Oh, I see."

He dashed into Charles' office, replaced the disc, and had another look at the Sandhurst photo. No doubt about it. He glanced out the window at the empty courtyard, took the image off the wall, and opened the scanner. He hit the button and watched the intense light pass under the frame.

Andrew's ear twitched as the outside door opened; more sweat formed on his brow. He hung the photo, checked it was straight and grabbed the printout.

Charles opened the door and ushered Dickie Phipps inside.

"I just stuck it back here for you. I was on my way when you called," Andrew babbled.

"Good, good. Thank you, Andrew," said Charles.

On his way out, Andrew exchanged pleasantries with Dickie and asked after his horses-in-training. He hopped on the quad and returned to his cottage for lunch, but he was not at all hungry. Andrew swore; the scan of the photo was spoiled from the glare of the glass. He would need to de-frame it and run off another copy. This would have to do for now. He found an envelope, scribbled a note on it and placed the e-mail and chip inside. Next, he placed everything into a larger padded bag, which he addressed. He'd post it tomorrow.

* * *

At five-thirty that evening, Andrew was leaning over Susan's desk checking a bill which Gary Holdsworth had returned unpaid.

Susan looked cross, she wanted to get home. "As you can see from his charming words, he claims that he doesn't recall giving approval for this." She scowled. "He's an awful little man. It'd give me the greatest pleasure to inform him that the bill stands."

Andrew exhaled despondently. "Me, too, but I've a feeling—" The desk phone rang, cutting him off.

"Good evening, Brockford Stud," chirped Susan. "Yes, sir. I'll just see if he's available."

Andrew's eyes wandered to the phone as Susan put the caller on hold. The screen displayed a long number; he had done enough research over the last month to recognise the Chinese dialling code.

Susan put the call through. Andrew desperately wanted to eavesdrop using her handset.

"There's a Mr. Ling on the line for you."

Charles sat bolt upright. "Put him straight through. Thank you, Susan."

"Ling, old chap! Good to hear from you! I take it your big conference was interesting and fruitful?"

"Good afternoon, Charles Buckham. It was, as you say, most

interesting. Overall, I bring you good news, though you may have to adjust your timeframe."

Charles grimaced. "Go on."

"I conducted exploratory meetings with some individuals who may be sympathetic to your vision. My suggestions were met with interest. Some even indicated their willingness to fully expand the betting service if the deal were, shall we say, *structured correctly...* But they all agree on one thing: Guo will never permit it. So we wait. He is not a young man and he has health problems. It is unlikely he will see out the full ten years of his Presidency. Patience, Charles, it will all happen in time."

"That's not at all what we discussed, Ling," he said, curling his hand into a fist.

"It is exactly what we discussed. It is the most prudent path to take and will ultimately result in success. Patience, Charles Buckham. Discuss it with Sir Piers, he will understand what I mean."

"I don't *have* time, you fucking little faggot. Make it happen this year or kiss goodbye to your career." Charles slammed the phone down, smashing the handset.

"Oh bollocks!" He flung the broken device at the filing cabinet. "Fuck! Fuck!" he said, as the phone clattered off the metal drawers.

He ran his hands through his hair and took a deep breath. Piers was right. Time to stop messing around. He wanted to call Rupert, and regretted his outburst with the telephone. He made for the door.

* * *

Andrew and Susan exchanged startled glances and looked at Charles' door. When the noise died down and he burst out, they stared, slack-jawed.

"What the hell are you two looking at?" he snapped.

Susan blinked and grabbed her bag. She never replied when Charles lost his temper. Andrew feebly asked, "Is everything OK?"

Charles fixed his cold beam on him. "What's it to you? Don't be so bloody nosey."

140

Andrew froze. Charles brushed past and slammed the door behind him.

"Charming," said Susan, putting on her coat. "I'm off home. Lock up, will you?"

Andrew was still a bit stunned as he found himself alone in the office. He stared at Charles' door and wondered.

* * *

The three ex-soldiers were discussing tactics in the private dining room of The Scimitar. When the waiter brought a fresh bottle of wine, they sat in silence until he left.

"So," began Charles. "Your little camera did the trick, Rupe. Andrew's not giving up. He took the disc and no doubt saw the footage – probably copied it. He also scanned our Sandhurst photo and printed off a couple of pages from my computer, but I'm not sure what exactly."

Piers cleared his throat. "Charlie, that's getting a bit close for comfort. Time for action, I'd say."

Charles had a pained expression. "I agree, except I don't want to lose him just yet."

"Oh come on, Charlie," said Rupert. "Stop dithering."

"Well, would you get rid of Goran on a whim?"

Rupert glanced at the door. The swarthy Serb was loitering outside, under orders. "If I had to, yes," he muttered. "But I see your point." He took a sip of wine and mulled things over.

"Anyway," said Charles. "On to the main order of business. Despite all our efforts, it seems that Ling's hit the political wall." He slammed a hand onto the table, making the cutlery rattle.

"Sounds like he needs a little incentive," said Rupert, grinning.

Piers folded his arms on the table and leaned closer. Rupert and Charles exchanged looks, their eyes sparkling as they felt a surge of adrenaline. They felt euphoric and nostalgic as they discussed the next phase.

Charles topped up the glasses. "Oh, by the way, Rupe, can you check out Andrew's friend, Jess Flint? She's a detective in the Met. I need to have something over him, something more than his job security and a fat bonus."

"Hmm, that's a tricky one. I'll go at it from another angle. I'm not about to have my people noticed sniffing around in police records."

"Don't tell me you can't get a minion to ask a few questions?"

"Not that simple, old boy. Unsurprisingly, the police don't much care for chaps like me. They're against the idea of firms like mine. They see us as a threat, afraid that the right kind of government might hand over more powers to us. Especially with this *wonderful* war on terror ticking away."

"Fuck the police, Rupe! If our plan comes together, chaps like you'll have *carte bloody blanche* to get what you want from the government."

Rupert grinned. "You're probably right, Charlie. I'll see what I can dig up. Oh, and don't worry, I know exactly what to do about your little dog." He told them what he had in mind.

Charles liked the idea, but suggested several refinements. Over dessert, they finalised the details.

Piers took it all in and gave it a seal of approval. If the grand plan worked and Slipstream expanded domestically, his shares would increase in value and he'd rent another 2,000 acres to Rupert for new training grounds. His red face shone with delight.

Chapter 22

Andrew's cottage, Brockford - One week later

Andrew flopped onto his sofa, showered and exhausted after another long shift on the stud.

Terry was out of action with a stomach bug, so Andrew had spent most of the previous night assisting a panicked Colin with a difficult foaling. After frantic manual adjustments, the foal was delivered and put on oxygen. A few hours later it rose and suckled as normal, much to everyone's relief. Before Andrew knew it, it was time for the morning coverings, and from then on, the day had been a blur of activity.

Too tired to read the *Racing Post*, he channel-surfed until he found a current affairs show debating the future of Chinese politics. He made himself a coffee and sat glued to the screen, tiredness suddenly banished to the back of his mind.

The consensus of the panel was that Guo Qingling would certainly take over the reins of power when the President stepped down. However, it was assumed that the conservative Guo would make little progress on human rights during his tenure.

Or gambling, thought Andrew, recalling Charles' rage the other evening.

There was speculation that if Guo's ally, Ling Jiao, was to step into the Vice President's office in October and eventually succeed Guo at the top, it could mark a sea-change in Chinese policy.

For Andrew, the documentary was a revelation. He realised that he could not keep burying his head in the sand of the breeding season. It was time for action.

If Charles bought the Tote this year and had a means of blackmailing the next Vice President, then... Andrew sat bolt upright. Charles was not a patient man.

A far-fetched idea crept into Andrew's head, but he dismissed it as ridiculous and the result of his exhaustion.

He yawned. Hopefully Terry would be back in action soon; it would be good to zip down to London and see Jess. There was so much to tell her.

His head was just hitting the pillow when the phone rang. To his relief, it was not another emergency. However, a conversation with Charles was hardly a better prospect.

"Don't tell me you're tired, Dixon. Bloody hell, I went weeks without a wink on the battlefield. No wonder you failed RCB."

Andrew rolled his eyes. He was sick of this shit. "Was that all you wanted to say?"

"Actually no, so you could perk up a bit. You're having dinner with us at The Scimitar tomorrow evening. Be there at eight. It's a celebration. Just us, Rupert and Piers."

"Celebrating what?"

"Our deal with the Tote and China! It'll be announced Ascot week. Everything's going ahead as planned and I haven't forgotten that I promised you a bonus."

"Oh, er, that's great. Brilliant. Thanks, but I don't know if I should come. Terry's sick. If there's a foaling, Colin'll need me. He's a bit panicked after the dystocia last night."

"Don't worry about that. Nothing's running milk, is it?"

"Well no, but that's not the point."

"God Almighty, I never thought I'd have to twist your arm for dinner at The Scimitar. You'll only be in Cambridge. In that car of yours, you can be back in 40 mins. And that's final."

"OK, see you tomorrow."

"Good, good." He hung up.

Andrew's head crashed to the pillow, he was asleep instantly.

* * *

The following morning, Jess was typing a report when her phone rang. She looked at Andrew's name on the screen. Smiling, she pressed the green button. "When you leave a note saying you'll call, that means in a month, does it? No wonder your posh girlfriends leave you."

"What? Oh, um, I've been flat out all hours. It's the breeding season, you know."

"Oh yeah, I forgot the whole world stops when the horses start shagging."

There was silence on the line.

Jess bit her lip. Maybe she'd overdone it?

"Sorry, Jess. You're right, but I did leave you a message."

She smiled. "Yeah, I know. Seriously, though, you need to take a breather: keep in touch with life."

He exhaled. "Funny, I've been thinking the exact same thing."

"I've been pretty busy myself. Late night surveillance and stuff. But at least I can get out on the bike and clear my head. When was the last time you went to Silverstone?"

He exhaled sharply. "December."

"Why don't you come down at the weekend? Have a few drinks and forget about stallions and selling horses."

"God, I'd love to. I've got plenty of news."

"Like what?"

"I've been doing a bit of, er, homework about Charles and his mates. They're up to something with the Chinese."

He told her all about the DVD.

"Hold on a sec." She glanced at her colleagues, left the office, and leaned against a car outside. "Are you telling me your boss is blackmailing the Chinese government? You're sure about this?"

"Jess, I've got a copy of the film. It's him, I know it. It has to be blackmail. Why else would Charles have it lying on his desk?"

"I take it Charles doesn't know you've seen the film?"

"I'm not stupid, Jess."

"Alright, alright. Where's your copy?"

"Safe."

"Can you get it to me."

"Yeah, I'll bring it down at the weekend."

"Good. Look, it's a start, but we need more than that."

"I'll see what I can find out tonight. Charles invited me to dinner at The Scimitar to celebrate the Tote deal."

"Bloody hell, that's posh."

"Yeah, Rupert and Piers'll be there, too. You know Rupert owns the place?"

"Really? Talk about going into the lions' den. Be careful."

"It's only dinner."

Jess started pacing back and forth. "Look, Andrew, assuming – worst case – everything you've told me is true. Then I don't think you should go."

"I don't have a choice, Jess. Charles is insisting. Hey, it could be interesting, I might find out a bit more when they're full of wine. Like you say: we need more information. Proof."

"Are you sure?"

"What can they do, lock me in the cellar? At least it's a public place, it's not like they can have me mugged or run over on their own doorstep."

She heard her name being called from an open window. "Oi, Flint, get yerself to the DCI's office."

"Look, Andrew I've got to go. I'm working tonight, but send me a text when you're home, OK?"

"Yes, ma'am!"

"Smartarse," she grinned. "Oh and Andrew."

"Yes?"

"Mind yourself. I wouldn't want… I mean, I… just make sure you let me know."

"Don't worry, Jess."

But she did.

Chapter 23

The Scimitar, Cambridge

That evening, when Andrew pulled up outside the restaurant, the valet took his car. Andrew did a double-take as he handed the guy a bank note. He was sure he had seen him before, at the wheel of Rupert's Maybach. Andrew went inside and gave his name to the hostess. He noticed the man who took his coat had closely cropped hair and military posture. The place was probably riddled with Slipstream employees. Andrew glanced at the door, but it was too late to do a runner. His palms were clammy as he was led to the private dining room.

The three ex-soldiers met him with smiles, handshakes, and pats on the back. Andrew took his place at the table as Charles handed out glasses of a rust-tinged drink.

"What's this?" asked Andrew, wrinkling his nose.

"Champagne cocktail," said Charles. "The perfect start to a celebration dinner."

"What's in it?"

"Bubbly, sugar lump, dash of brandy. Proper stuff," said Rupert, taking a sip of his own. "Come on. Chin, chin, Andrew."

Andrew caught Charles staring at him and put his glass down. "I'd better stick to beer. Got to drive home."

"Nonsense," said Piers. "One glass won't do you any harm."

"I wouldn't have bothered to invite you if I'd known you'd be such a wet fart. Drink up for Christ's sake," said Charles.

"Alright, just the one then." Andrew picked up his glass.

"Gentlemen," said Charles. "To China, and to British racing."

"To China," they said in unison.

Andrew sipped the fizzy liquid and winced from the bitter taste. He thought it'd be a struggle to finish his glass, but after a few minutes of horsey small talk, the concoction steadied his nerves. He found himself sipping rapidly until his glass was dry. Charles offered to make him a refill.

"No thanks better not. I'll have a light beer."

Charles glanced at his watch. "Right you are. I suppose it's time to order," he said.

Piers nodded. Rupert stood. "I'll get our waiter," he said, leaving the room.

Rupert closed the door behind him and snapped his fingers. A waiter came scurrying. "Go and take the orders," he said, pulling out his phone. He clicked the stopwatch on his Rolex and made the call.

"Give the injection in exactly fifteen minutes." He disconnected and dialled again. "It's me. I've got a name for you. Flint, Jess. Probably short for Jessica. Get her details from the DVLA, then find a mobile number for her. She's a copper, so be careful... Yes, good. I want the full package. ASAP." He hung up and rejoined the others.

* * *

Victor crouched in the darkness. He watched the man walk along the foaling unit, checking each stable. After closing the last door, the man disappeared around the back of the building. Mr. Calcott had said the guy did his rounds every ten minutes or so. Victor checked the luminous dial on his watch. It was time.

He slid his black-clad form out of the shadows and dashed silently through the beam of the yard light. Third door from the left. As he opened the latch, he pulled off his balaclava and remembered what they had told him: no sudden movements around the horses. In the stable, he dropped his shoulders and kept his eyes down.

The horse was munching hay; she flicked her ears and snorted gently. Victor carefully reached out and stroked her neck, working his way to her head. The mare stopped eating and leaned into his caress. He grabbed the headcollar and pulled the small syringe from his pocket. Keeping a tight hold, he firmly jabbed the needle into the mare's neck. She flinched slightly, but did not pull away. The oxytocin went straight into her system. Victor closed the door quietly, ran back to the trees, and sent a text message while he waited for the man to check the horses again.

When the action started, he would creep over to Andrew's cottage.

* * *

Outside The Scimitar, Goran sidled up to the green Lotus. Silently, he opened the door and stashed the small bag under the seat. Then, he put the tiny LED light on his head and dropped to the ground. He pulled the long industrial needle from his jacket and rolled under the car. He found the brake lines easily enough, but had to grope for a moment to locate the power steering system. The needle pierced a clean hole in each. Nothing large or noticeable, but with speed and pressure, the leaks would start. He extricated himself, went to the Maybach, and sent a text message.

* * *

Andrew pushed the remainder of his beer away, he was starting to feel a bit lightheaded. He cursed himself for drinking the cocktail.

"Anyway," said Charles. "I want to thank you for keeping your ears open and mouth shut about the Tote thing. It's as good as signed and sealed."

"Er, that's great news. So, um, when will you get the Chinese simulcast rights?"

Andrew watched the three ex-soldiers exchange looks. He noticed Charles shrug almost imperceptibly, before replying. "Oh, I should imagine it'll all be in the bag by October."

"What makes you so sure?" said Andrew. "Did they give it to you in writing?"

"When one deals with the Chinese," said Piers, "it's all about the connections one has and how one uses them. They call it *Guanxi*."

"And you've got them?"

"Oh yes, we've got them," snorted Rupert. "Exactly where we want them." He checked his watch, looking slightly annoyed.

"Listen, I was thinking," said Charles, in a jovial tone. "When I send you to Beijing on reconnaissance, you can take that girl of yours with you. Flint, isn't it?"

Andrew's stomach flipped. "I told you, she's just a friend. It's… we're—"

Rupert laughed. "You can't fool us, Dixon. A trip to China and a night in a former Imperial Palace'll get her knickers off; guaranteed. But if you want to have her at home, I could book you a table here. Always works for—" His phone beeped, cutting him off. He checked it. "Ah! Spot on," he said, cutting a sideways glance at Charles.

Andrew had a strange feeling. A sort of shiver ran up his neck and over the top of his head, making him feel happy. His skin tingled. He rubbed his face with his hands and felt his jaw twitch. His brain went off on a tangent: imagining him and Jess walking along the Great Wall, laughing and joking. Then his phone rang.

He answered and it snapped him back to reality with a jolt. Colin could barely get the words out. "Andrew, where are you? Melodic Maiden's foaling. Only one leg coming."

Andrew went pale. "What? She's not due for nearly a month."

"Well, she's lying in front of me straining like she's going to burst an artery."

"A problem?" said Charles, with a look of concern.

Andrew ignored Charles. He rubbed his forehead and tried to focus. He knew he shouldn't have left the farm. "Colin, get her up and keep her walking. I'm on my way. Oh, and Colin, don't panic and do anything stupid." He hung up. Suddenly feeling parched, he downed a glass of water and looked at Charles. "Melodic Maiden's gone into early labour. I'm off."

"Oh gosh! That's one of Tony Fowler's mares. Go on, quick as you can. Don't let anything happen to her."

Andrew dashed out. While the valet brought his car, he called the vet and explained the problem. Seconds later, he swung onto the A14 dual carriageway and floored the accelerator. Nine pm on a Wednesday evening, traffic was light, but he didn't need to get pulled over. He backed off and held the car at sixty-five.

He felt thirsty again, but hadn't any water. He licked his lips and found himself chewing his gums. He looked at the speedometer, realised he was up to eighty-five again. Back to sixty-five. The brakes felt a bit sluggish. Must get the car serviced. He was glad he didn't finish that beer.

Another shiver passed through his scalp. Jess. He should call Jess; there was so much to tell her. He felt a rush of pleasure as he pictured her on the sofa wearing her pearl earrings. She was the only woman who had ever understood him. He took several deep breaths. Another shiver – a rush. More powerful this time. His train of thought faltered, like a needle slipping on a record.

He was puzzled by the gang of three's niceness. Were they trying to buy him off? Why? They couldn't know he'd seen the film. Charles said they'd be sorted by October. Why October?

Once again Andrew saw he was hitting ninety and slowed down, checking his mirrors. Brakes definitely needed more fluid. Just his luck: two problem foalings in as many nights. If Colin kept her walking until he arrived, it would work out alright. Another intense wave of energy erupted through him, his heart was pounding. He put the radio on and tapped his hands to the beat. He was buzzing.

An image of Piers crept into his head. The *horse flied lice* e-mail spun round in his mind. *I say, if the little poofter can't get it done, instead of the pool footage, why not give it the Anatolian shove.* October. That was it. Ling would take office in October, but what about?

Then he understood. The deal was going to go ahead alright. At any cost.

How could he stop them? Jess. Jess was great. She would know. Andrew could feel his heart thumping.

Just then, one of his favourite songs came on the radio. He turned up the volume and kicked on as Jessie J blasted through 'Price Tag'.

Andrew shot past Newmarket and merged onto the A11, the speedometer edging over ninety. The steering felt stiff, like a real racecar. Andrew focused on the road. He was flying, at one with the machine. Traffic was still light, but each time he passed a car, the rear lights seemed to glow. Vividly. It was like he was in a nightclub. Music engulfed him. The oncoming headlights were dancing, almost flashing. His gums were getting sore, why was he chewing them? He never usually did that. Sweat dripped off him. God, he was thirsty. No time to stop for a drink. The poor horse. Colin would be in a state, too.

He passed the turn for Chestnut Close housing estate, he would soon be upon Thetford Forest roundabout. Then straight to Brockford: the mare was going to be fine. "Yesss!" he roared. He would get there before the vet. In fact, *everything* was going to be fine. He had never felt like this before, he was... He couldn't describe it, but it felt so good.

Jess. God, he was an idiot. It was right there all the time. She was the one for him. He loved her. He needed to tell her that.

Music blared. Now there were blue lights flashing. They looked cool. Where? In the mirror. Shit, he was doing well over a hundred. He didn't need this right now. He would explain it was a veterinary emergency. He jabbed at the brake, the pedal went limp under his foot. Not good. The blue lights were closer now. Ahead, he could make out the large tree-dotted roundabout. Panicking, he changed gear and tried the brakes again. Nothing. The steering was so stiff. Trees, and blue lights. Jess. What was happening? His brain was frazzled.

Andrew felt the car hit the kerb. The seatbelt cut into his shoulder. Everything slowed down. The car lifted into the air like it was floating. He thought of his parents, and Jess. Then pain screamed through him.

The policemen felt their car sway when the Lotus flashed past.

"Fucking 'ell, Ayrton Senna's back from the dead," said Sergeant Hardy. He turned on the siren and set off in pursuit.

Mike Atherton called it in. Another unit would meet them on the forest road.

"Get the plates. Run 'em. He's doing over a hundred. It's early in the week for sodding joyriders," said Hardy, desperately trying to gain on the runaway.

"Doesn't look like he's slowing for the roundabout," said Atherton. "God, if he hits someone."

Hardy punched the brakes. Ahead, the Lotus slowed a bit, but not enough. Hardy's jaw dropped open as he watched the light sportscar hit the low barrier and flip into the air. Its rear end rose up, giving the policemen a clear view of the undercarriage. It slammed into the large oak tree, like a pie slapped onto a wall. There was a loud bang and the sound of twisting metal.

Hardy screeched his car to a halt. "Call an ambulance and a fire crew, then seal off the road," he barked at Atherton.

Hardy left the lights flashing and trotted over to the wreck. Its wheels still spun and it rested at a sixty-degree angle to the ground; rear end mashed onto the tree, bonnet jammed into the earth. Hardy shone his torch at the hole where the window should have been. He screwed up his face and sucked air between his teeth. One bloodied occupant suspended by the seatbelt.

Atherton came up behind him. "Ambulance and firemen'll be here in five," he said, inspecting the damage with a grimace. "What's that you said about Ayrton Senna?"

Chapter 24

Atherton and Hardy watched the ambulance roar away. The wreckage had been attached to a crane and was being hoisted back onto its wheels. The driver's door had been cut off and lay on the ground at their feet. The area was cordoned off and four more policemen ushered cars past the scene. People rubbernecked, hoping to catch a glimpse of something grisly.

The mangled car was placed carefully on the road, and the firemen informed Hardy their work was done.

"Cheers, mate. The tow truck's on its way. We'll handle it from here," said the policeman. He turned to Atherton. "Right, gloves on."

Hardy held the torch, while Atherton carefully reached inside the wreck. Stuffed in the sun visor, he found the DVLA log book and a driver's licence.

"The system said the vehicle's registered to an Andrew Dixon," said Atherton. "Log book confirms it and the licence is his." He handed the documents to Hardy.

"Huh. Bloody idiot." Hardy frowned. "Hang on a sec, I met him out at Brockford Hall. I was there a while back, somebody threw a bucket of blood at the front door. I interviewed Dixon."

"One of Lord Nancy's boys, was he?"

"No. He worked for the brother. Ran the stud farm. His dad was that banker that was all over the news. Remember?"

Atherton shrugged. "Give us the torch, Sarge."

Hardy handed it over and Atherton checked the interior. He was about to get to his feet, when the beam caught something bright wedged between the seat and the console.

Atherton fished out the small bag and examined it. He counted twenty-seven pills. They were an off-white colour, flecked with bright blue and stamped with the emblem of a dove. "You naughty boy," he muttered.

"Whatcha got there?" said Hardy.

"Well, I'll bet you a pint they ain't aspirin," he said, brandishing the bag.

"Ecstasy." Hardy shook his head in disgust. "Idiot. I'm sick of these rich arseholes thinking the law doesn't apply to 'em. Racing his car with a head full of pills? If he survives, I'll throw the fucking book at 'im."

Somewhere nearby, a phone rang. Hardy whipped his head around. "Where's that coming from?" Then he saw it, flashing on the grass near the tree. He picked up the damaged smartphone.

"You gonna answer it?" asked Atherton.

Hardy held up the device. "Can't. Screen's cracked. Whatever happened to good old fashioned keypads, eh?"

Jess let it ring until it went to voicemail, she left Andrew a brief message. An uneasy feeling nagged her. She sipped her tea from the plastic cup and kept her eyes on the warehouse, but her mind was elsewhere. A few minutes later, she sent Andrew a text and hoped he would reply.

Later that night, Atherton was typing out the incident report. The bag of ecstasy and the phone sat on his desk. It rang again. He gave it a sideways glance. "Fourth time since I sat down," he said to the device. "You're persistent, whoever you are."

It rang again, immediately. Atherton picked up the phone and inspected the damaged screen. He could not decipher the name. He swiped his finger several times across the screen. It kept ringing. He swiped one more time and the phone went silent. He was about to put it down, when he heard a muffled voice. Gingerly, he put the phone to his ear.

"Andrew!" said the voice. "I've been worried sick. Don't you dare do that to me again."

"I'm sorry, madam. This is Constable Atherton, Norfolk Constabulary, Thetford police station. Could I have your name, please?"

"What? Where's Andrew Dixon? What's going on?"

"I'm sorry, madam, I need your name before I can divulge any—"

"This is Detective Sergeant Jessica Flint, Metropolitan Police Service, Wembley. Collar number: four-seven-quebec-kilo. Andrew Dixon is a personal friend of mine. Constable Atherton, I suggest you tell me what's going on."

Atherton immediately regretted his curiosity. He cleared his throat and told her what he knew.

There was silence on the line.

"He was taken to Cambridge, Addenbrookes," Atherton added, hastily.

"I'll be with you in the morning. Let the duty officer know I'll be coming, and have all the evidence and paperwork laid out for me," she said in a quivering voice. "I want prints run off that bag of pills."

Atherton said he would.

Jess hung up. Tears fell down her cheek. She batted them away, took a deep breath, and called Andrew's parents.

Chapter 25

The following morning, Lesley Grimsby pulled into the driveway of the Fellowes' home for another day of cleaning and cooking. She noticed the Bentley in front of the garage door. Strange, she thought, as she parked behind the house. Mr. Fellowes never left it outside overnight.

The newspapers were still at the back door, wrapped in plastic. Lesley frowned and let herself into the pantry. She checked the kitchen, but the usual aroma of tea and toast was absent. It wasn't like Mr. Fellowes to sleep in. She tried his office: nobody.

"Mr. Fellowes! Are you there?" she called, as she climbed the stairs. An uneasy feeling shot through her. He really hadn't been himself since Mrs. Fellowes passed. Lesley got to the top landing and heard a sharp crack from the master bedroom. She froze, hand on the doorknob. For a second she considered running downstairs, then she heard the noise again.

Taking a breath, she knocked and called; "Mr. Fellowes," in a nervous croak.

Nothing. Then another sharp crack.

Lesley turned the handle and pushed open the door. She edged into the room and saw the empty bed. The sheets were dragged down, not neatly turned back like usual. He must've got up in a hurry. There was another crack. She stared at the bathroom door. Gulping, she moved gingerly through the room and took another deep breath when her hand touched the bathroom doorknob. Another crack. She jumped. The noise seemed to snap through her. Heart thumping, she eased her way into the bathroom.

To her relief, she saw the teak-framed window swinging.

Another gust of wind slammed it closed. Lesley smiled and scolded herself for being so stupid. She went to close the latch and the uneasy feeling rose in her gut again. Chewing her lip, she stole a downwards glance out the window. There was nothing below except gravel and lawn.

Lesley made her way back to the kitchen. She frowned. Where was he? Perhaps he had gone for a walk around the fields. Yes, that must be it. She put the kettle on and fanned out the papers on the table. Then she went to the living room to clean out the fireplace. She swept up, put the ashes on the compost heap, and went back to the pantry. Lesley checked her watch; she might as well set the fire now. She opened the door connecting the house to the garage and stepped into the darkness to get tinder and logs. She fumbled for the light switch. The empty space flooded with yellow light. Out of the corner of her eye, she saw something moving. Shifting her eyes to the object, she dropped the bucket and screamed.

Two hours later, Lesley sat at the kitchen table. She was pale, shaking, and trying to calm herself with sweet, milky tea. Policemen crawled all over the property, searching for a note or anything else unusual. Lesley was vaguely aware that she was answering questions, but the image of Mr. Fellowes dangling from the beam was seared onto her retinas.

The policeman explained that her employer had apparently attached himself to the electric pulley system and pressed the remote control. As the door closed, it hoisted him over the beam and into the air. Lesley ran for the toilet and vomited.

The police called her son, who said he'd leave work and bring his mother home.

Like all the rubberneckers, Goran drove slowly past the house. He counted an ambulance, two police cars, and a fire crew. He continued for another mile before he pulled over and called his boss.

Chapter 26

Addenbrookes Hospital, Cambridge

Andrew's mind swam out of the depths. It was time to surface and face the world again. As he slowly opened his eyes, the light stung his retinas. He was weak, so very weak. He tried to sit up, but there was something attached to his hand. Where was he? In a bed. How did he get here? Was there somebody there? Jess? He plummeted into darkness again.

A bright light shone in his eyes. There was a man standing over him, talking.

"…Dr. Wilso… You've been throu…" There was somebody beside him. Jess? Mum?

"…Andrew, I…"

Darkness again.

The next time light invaded his senses, he was able to focus. He moved his neck, looked about. Hospital room. His mother was there, asleep in a chair. No sign of Jess.

Andrew moved his lips, but his words were silent. Then he heard himself. "Mum. Where am I? How long?" He felt so weary.

Then he saw her stand and smile. She looked different somehow. Her hair was immaculate, but she wasn't as thin and tanned as he remembered. Pale, but not shrivelled. She looked healthier.

"Thank God," she said, kissing him on the cheek. "I've been out of my mind. They weren't sure how long it would last. How do you feel?"

His mother smelled different, too. "Mum, what are you talking about? How long..? What would?" Then it occurred to him: she

159

didn't smell of alcohol. He checked the room again. "Where's Dad?"

"Oh, I told him not to come. It's bad enough the papers having a go at you, without him being seen here."

Andrew eased himself up in the bed. He felt like he'd had the worst ever fall off a horse. "What? Mum, I don't..." he mumbled, frowning. "Have you been drinking?"

She ran her hand through his hair. "I haven't had a drop since Jess called me that awful night."

"Really?"

"Yes, really."

He smiled, relieved. "That's great. How long have I been here?"

She looked apprehensive. "I'll get your doctor," she said, pulling the door open.

Andrew let out a long breath and fell back into oblivion.

He woke again. Maybe a minute later, maybe an hour, the doctor was standing with his mother.

"Andrew, I'm Dr. Wilson. You were admitted here with a linear fracture of the skull. The CT scan revealed mild sub-cranial bleeding. We operated and induced a coma to assist healing. Do you remember what happened to you?"

Andrew frowned, searching his mind. His mother started to speak, but Dr. Wilson raised his hand.

"I was driving back to the farm," said Andrew. "I... there was a mare foaling, I was in a rush to help her. Did I crash?"

Wilson nodded.

"Oh God. Did I hit anyone?"

"You hit a tree. No other cars were involved. Now then, Andrew. How many fingers am I holding up?"

"Two."

"Follow them, please." He swept his hand across Andrew's field of vision.

"Good. Excellent. How old are you, Andrew?"

"Thirty."

Wilson continued with a series of questions about Andrew's life. Andrew answered them slowly. His head throbbed.

"Doctor, how long have I been here?"

Wilson picked up the chart. "Let's see. You were admitted March 28th. Today's the first of June. So, just over nine weeks. Your memory is remarkably good, all things considered."

Andrew was stunned. "You kept me in a coma for nine weeks?"

"Actually, we kept you under for three. Your body took care of the rest all by itself. You're a very lucky man," said Wilson.

There was something in Wilson's eyes. It was a look Andrew had seen many times before: barely concealed disapproval. He could do without his father's legacy at the moment.

"Right," said Wilson. "I'll leave you two alone, but not too much talking. You need to take it easy. Your body has been through quite an ordeal. You need time to get strong. We'll monitor your progress daily, with a view to discharge in a fortnight or so."

"Thank you, Doctor," said Andrew.

Wilson gave him a tight smile and left.

Fenella Dixon sat on the bed and took her son's hand. "I'm so glad you're awake. I was out of my mind with worry."

"Mum, I–"

She squeezed his hand. "Please, dear, let me finish."

Andrew nodded.

"I know I've been out of my mind in another way for many years, but that's over. I even went to a meeting or two, but I found them rather sordid. I don't need a support group; I simply don't want to drink any more."

"Good for you."

They smiled at each other.

"When Jess called me that night, I was blotto. I hardly knew what she was talking about. Never again. I don't want to miss any more of life."

"That's great, Mum, it really is."

His mother looked uneasy; she opened her mouth as if to speak. Eventually, she found the words. "Andrew, I know I haven't been the best example to you. I spent most of my time trying to blot out your father's disgrace. But, I never imagined you'd turn to drugs to deal with it."

"Drugs? I don't do drugs. Why would you think that?"

"They found ecstasy in your car and your bloodstream, dear."

Andrew's jaw fell open. "That's absurd. I don't touch the stuff."

"They say, at those meetings, that you can't get over it until you admit it."

"I have nothing to admit."

"It's OK, dear."

"So you don't believe me?"

"My dear Andrew, I never knew it'd gotten so bad for you. Perhaps I would have, if I'd been on this planet," she sighed. "That's another reason I stopped."

Andrew desperately tried to recall the night of his crash; dinner at The Scimitar, Charles, Piers and Rupert. They were… His head was throbbing now. He felt thirsty, reached for the glass by his bed, and downed it in one.

"Where's my phone?"

"It was damaged in the crash. The rest of your things are in that locker with some new clothes."

He nodded. "Mum, I need to see Jess. It's urgent. Can you get hold of her?"

"She'll be here soon, I expect. She's been an absolute rock, you know. She doesn't believe you took drugs. Simply won't hear of it. She was livid when the papers found out and went to town on you."

"I've been in the papers?"

She looked grave. "I'm afraid so."

"Mum, I sent you an envelope. Where is it?"

She gestured to the bedside locker. "It's with your clothes and washbag. Very cloak-and-dagger. What's in it?"

"Just get Jess. Please." Andrew exhaled and crashed back onto the pillows. Sleep was welcome and deep.

* * *

"Yeah, thanks for calling Fenella," said Jess. "I'll be up tonight." A smile spread across her whole face for the first time since it happened.

She turned on the engine and pulled out into the London

traffic. And then she saw him in the mirror. Same guy, same black Ducati. He'd been there, off and on, ever since she'd started asking questions about that suicide. He was making it obvious, that was for sure. Unless he was a complete amateur, and she doubted that. The bike followed her to the station and roared past when she turned in.

The time she went to her DCI and asked for back-up to nab the guy, he didn't show for ten days. Typical; it made her a laughing stock.

Then her superiors told her to stop wasting her time on a suicide up in Suffolk, and everyone took the piss out of her for getting upset over a druggie toff.

* * *

When Andrew woke, golden sunlight filled the room. He was alone. He felt bright and clear, though still very weak. He rubbed his eyes and saw the small present on the bedside locker. He opened it and took out the brand new smartphone. There was no note. He smiled and looked around: Jess. She was great. Where was she hiding?

Andrew eased himself out of bed, he could barely stand. A nurse came in and berated him for getting up unassisted.

"Have you seen my visitor?" he asked her.

"No, I haven't. Now, take this to steady you." She placed a zimmerframe in front of him. "Toilet's first on the left."

"Thanks." Feeling embarrassed, he rattled his way down the hall. When he got back, he collapsed on the bed, knackered.

He heard the door close and looked up. His heart nearly stopped.

Charles stood there. Arms folded. Eyes cut into Andrew like lasers.

"I see you got my present," he said.

Andrew couldn't speak.

"I thought I'd give you a nice new one. You can kill time and keep in touch with the world, while you're stuck in here. I spoke to your doctor. Nice chap. Says you'll be out in a few weeks. I'll expect you back at work soon after that. Terry's been holding the fort on the farm, but he can't run the business like you."

Andrew's mouth was dry.

Charles sat on the end of the bed. Andrew shuffled away from him.

Charles cleared his throat. "Pity about George Fellowes. Wasn't it?" he said.

Andrew shook his head, his brow knitted. "Come again?"

"Bloody old fool topped himself." Charles kept his icy gaze on Andrew. "He was quite mad, you know, spouting all sorts of wild nonsense to anybody who'd listen. Some might say he had it coming – and they'd be right." He pulled his face into a cheery smile. "Well, anyway, I'm glad you survived. It could've gone either way for you."

Andrew grabbed a fist of bedsheet; he wanted to hit Charles.

Charles watched him get angry. He laughed for a second, then froze his features into a dark scowl. "Look here, Dixon," he spat, jabbing a finger at Andrew. "Don't you ever go through my affairs again. Don't concern yourself with my business and never, ever try to get into my office. I've had a keypad lock installed. Furthermore, you will never access my e-mails again. Or the next time, you might not escape with your life. Oh, and don't even think of going to the police. We're watching Miss Flint. It would be tragic if she collided with a truck on one of her dawn cycles, wouldn't it?"

"You won't get away with—"

"Shut the fuck up. Your credibility's in tatters. People think you're as cavalier as your father. *Arrogant, joy-riding, druggie toff*, was what one paper called you. Others weren't as kind."

"I've never done drugs in my life. You slipped me a Mickey Finn in that bloody cocktail."

Charles roared with laughter. "You sound like a jockey, or one of those footballers." He leaned in close. "Don't worry, I'll keep you on at Brockford and you'll make just enough to scrape by, but there'll be no more bonuses. You're my little soldier, and don't you ever forget it." He looked at his watch. "Is that the time? Must be off. We'll chat again later." He strode out.

Andrew picked up the phone. He was about to call Jess when he remembered the envelope. He checked the locker. It was still there, sealed. He looked at the phone like it was poisonous. Where was Jess?

He stared at the ceiling, thinking, for the rest of the afternoon. That evening, he ate every morsel of the bland hospital food. He was going to need his strength, that much he knew. Andrew replayed the events of that fateful night over and over. The details were blurry. Eventually his mind drifted, but an uneasy feeling nagged him like a splinter. He took out the envelope, opened it, and re-read the e-mails. He placed everything under his pillow and massaged his scalp. The scar was itchy. He yawned and pulled the covers up.

* * *

"Andrew," said Jess, squeezing his hand. "How're you feeling?"

"Better now," he said, with a goofy smile. He felt his heart thumping.

She wagged her finger at him. "You had us worried, you know that?"

"So Mum says." He glanced at the door. "She said they found drugs in my system. Is that true?"

"Yeah," she paused, chewing her lip. "Ecstasy. I saw the tox report. And they found twenty-seven pills in your car. That's possession with intent. Ten to fifteen years. The fuckers got you good."

"You know that's not me, right?"

"Yeah. Trouble is, nobody else does. I ran prints on the bag. They're not yours, but they didn't find a match. Still, at least they're in the system. If we can print Charles or the others, we might get lucky."

"Huh. Some chance." Andrew snorted. "You know, even Mum doesn't believe me. The doctor gives me dirty looks, too. Mum said it's been in the papers."

She sighed. "Yeah. Look, after the crash, I went to Thetford station and spoke to them. The Sergeant that found you wanted to throw the book at you. I tried to talk him down, but he wasn't having it. He charged you when you were out cold. Your mum didn't have the cash, so I posted your bail, but I'm going to need to give them your passport now you're awake. You want me to get you a lawyer?" she said, her voice cracking.

He nodded gravely. "Suppose you'd better."

"There's something else," she said. Her words hung in the air.

"Go on, then," said Andrew, looking resigned.

"George Fellowes committed suicide."

"I know. Charles came to see me yesterday." He frowned and winced as the pain ran over his temple. "Or maybe it was this morning." He told her all about it and she told him about her stalker.

"Holy shit, Jess."

"You shouldn't use that new phone." She produced her own handset. "Wouldn't surprise me if they got mine tapped and tagged, too. It's pretty easy if you've got Calcott's resources . I'll get us disposables. We can't fuck around any more, Andrew." She stared at the floor. "I saw Fellowes' body after the postmortem. Coroner said his injuries were consistent with suicide. These guys are professionals."

There was an urgency in her eyes that Andrew had never seen before. Fear crept up his spine. "SAS training; best in the world," he said. "If they catch us nosing around, we're dead."

"That's not all. The Chief Super in Suffolk gave me a dressing down for interfering with the suicide case and when I told my DCI about Charles and the gang, he thought I'd lost it. Makes me wonder if they've got connections in the Force. What are we going to do, Andrew?"

He looked lost. "I don't know, but time's running out. They told me the Tote deal'll be done by Ascot week and the Chinese gambling thing'll be sorted in October. They were bragging about it, and see, the Chinese leadership changes in October. Ling'll be the new vice-president. Apparently, he's a sure thing. And they've got him in their pocket."

"There'll be no stopping them…" Her voice trailed off.

Andrew had a flashback, he clicked his fingers. "The next President'll be no pushover, though. He's conservative and anti-gambling." He stopped suddenly, a blank look plastered on his face.

"What?" asked Jess.

"Wish I could remember. We're missing something. Rupert told me they'd got them right where they wanted them."

"He pulled the envelope out of the locker and tossed it on her lap. "This is what I have. Watch the footage, keep it safe. There's stuff in my cottage, too. There's a spare key under a brick outside the back door. Call Susan, use my passport as your excuse. You'll find a small packet taped under the sink in the kitchen. It's a copy of the Sandhurst picture and a bunch of phone numbers. You'll need to enter them all on my disposable, in case we have to go at it another way."

She nodded. "Does Charles know you've copied the footage?"

Andrew shook his throbbing head. "He didn't mention it. Anyway, I don't think he cares either way. He's got me where he wants me." He yawned. "God, I'm knackered already."

Jess squeezed his hand again. "You have a sleep," she gave him a peck on the cheek. "I'll stay till your mum gets here."

"Jess, I… Look, there's something I need to tell you. I, I've—" he felt like a silly teenager.

Grinning, she put a finger to his lips. "Later, Andrew. Later."

He drifted off again.

* * *

Goran was alone on the number two firing range at Slipstream headquarters. He wore a bespoke black coat, cut wide in the waist to conceal his weapon. The sky was mottled grey and the Scottish wind howled. He disliked British summers, but he was glad of the challenging conditions while he trained.

The AS-Val Silent Compact Sniper Rifle hung under his left arm, hidden by the long coat. The targets were 300 metres away. He paced over and back, jumped up and down. The weapon remained secure. After a few deep breaths, he pressed his stopwatch and pulled the short gun into view, flipping open its stock in one deft movement. He grinned. Old Soviet weapons were unbeatable. Simple, efficient, effective. The Serb had first used the AS when he was just nineteen, crouched like a panther on the rooftops of Pristina. Even then, it had felt like part of him.

Goran snapped a ten-round clip into place and leaned on the table. He fixed the crosshairs on the target and regulated his breathing. The weapon coughed six sub-sonic rounds in as many seconds. Satisfied, he stripped the gun, placed it in the custom-made boxes at his feet and stopped the clock. A fraction over ninety seconds. His best time yet. He used his binoculars to double-check the targets. Each one had two shots to the chest. Perfect. He pressed the control button. When the targets began moving, he repeated the drill, scoring more direct hits.

It was going to be easy.

Chapter 27

Charles, Rupert and Piers sat in the library at Brockford. With Jamie in London, they had the place to themselves. A thick folder of legal documents lay on the side table; Charles admired it like a trophy. They were now the proud owners of the Tote.

"Final phase underway," said Charles. "I gave the phone to Dixon. That means we've got a track on both of them. If either comes within spitting distance, we'll know."

"Oh, we'll know more than that," said Rupert. "With the gear I put on that little thing, it's like having him bugged. As long as it's turned on, my team'll hear everything the microphone can, even when he's not on a call."

"Bloody hell," said Piers. "Are you serious?"

"Absolutely."

"Gosh, that's a nice little bonus," said Charles. "What about Flint?"

"No. Only calls, messages and positioning."

Charles pursed his lips. "Pity."

"Why not just knock her off altogether?" said Rupert.

"Are you mad, Rupe? Apart from the inherent dangers in knocking off a London police officer on the eve of our biggest operation, I don't want a grieving Dixon turning into another George Fellowes," said Charles.

"Hmm, fair point."

"We're not in the desert any more. Besides, when the dust has settled and I've found a replacement for Dixon, you can knock them both off."

169

Rupert grinned and cracked his knuckles.

"OK, chaps," said Piers. "I've pulled a few strings to get press passes for the men, but I can't swing proper tickets at such short notice."

"Not to worry, we'll arrive early and use the men to bring the wine inside. They can lay low until it's time."

"Good idea, Charlie," said Piers.

"You'll have to be there, too, Piers. You can pull rank if we get any abuse from security."

"Don't worry," said Piers grinning.

"Rent-a-mob's already demonstrating," said Rupert. "They'll step it up a notch at the right time to provide a distraction."

"Good, good. We're all set," said Charles, a twinkle in his eye.

"Right." Rupert stood up. "I'm off to Baghdad. Back Sunday night. See you chaps on D-Day." He looked jubilant.

Chapter 28

Andrew finished his press-ups. He could now complete four sets of sixty every day, and felt fit and ready to check out. The headaches had almost disappeared, and his doctor had scheduled him for a final scan next Tuesday.

He did not want to return to Brockford.

Pulling a smile onto his face, he wandered into the main ward to watch the morning news.

Onscreen, a reporter stood outside Parliament and the words *Chinese delegation to arrive for Monday talks,* scrolled across the picture.

He turned up the sound.

The Business Secretary, Mr. Grounding, remains tight-lipped, saying only, 'we expect to be able to make a formal statement on Monday evening at the scheduled press conference'.

Chinese Vice-President Guo Qingling and Prime Minister Brookson are expected to sign bilateral trade agreements reportedly worth over one billion pounds, giving British companies greater access to Chinese markets. It is expected that a ban on British poultry exports to China, in place since a 2007 avian flu outbreak, is to be lifted. Educational and cultural relationships will also be on the agenda. It is thought that the number of Chinese attending our universities will increase significantly.

UK exports to China have increased by 18% since Mr. Brookson took office, and there are high hopes that this new 'landmark' agreement will see British businesses branch out of Beijing and Shanghai and

171

into the rapidly developing provincial cities.

The reporter glanced behind her: *Activists demonstrating on the bridge are demanding talks on human rights and the occupation of Tibet. A Downing Street representative recently stated that in such matters, 'both nations need to respect each other and refrain from finger-pointing', citing dialogue as the solution.*

Andrew rushed to his room and called Jess. "Yeah, it's me. Have you seen the news?"

"No?"

He told her. "I get it now. That is, I got it that night, racing back to Brockford: they're going to kill Guo Qingling."

"Are you nuts? That's a step up from the BHA chairman."

"Yes, but it's worth it to Charles. Think about it: with Guo gone, Ling'll be President in October. And they'll own him."

Jess was silent.

"Are you there?" said Andrew.

"Yeah. Don't worry, I'll get myself sent to Whitehall."

"Jess, what if I call the papers today? Show them the footage, expose Ling and implicate Charles. It'd make killing Guo pointless, right?"

"No, mate. If the press publishes in time – and it's a big if – Charles'll fucking wriggle out of it. Guys like him always do. And they might kill Guo anyway. We'll just ruin Ling's career. And it's not his fault he's gay," she said. "Oh yeah, and we'll probably have tragic accidents in the next year or so."

"Hmmm. I suppose you're right. Well, I'm going to make one phone call anyway."

"You sure? That's risky – Charles'll find out."

"I've got to try it."

"Please, don't do it. It's our last resort. Wait, Andrew. I'm on the job."

* * *

"Can you really be sure your 'friends' will act in such a way?" asked Ling's wife.

Ling grinned at her. A twinkle in his eye. "It is in their nature, my dear. They simply cannot help themselves." He took her hand in his and rubbed his thumb on her palm. "They merely think of their own interests, and thus, such a course of action becomes not only acceptable, but necessary. When they succeed, they imagine that they will benefit, but they have not stopped to consider the true outcome."

She arched her brow, shooting him a sideways look.

Ling chuckled. "In the aftermath, China will receive a great deal of political leeway."

She smiled, nodding. "*Carte blanche*, perhaps."

"Just like the Americans after 9/11."

Chapter 29

Jess stood in the glass-walled office feeling like a schoolgirl before the headmaster.

DCI Barlow stared at his computer. Jess chewed her nails. Barlow was stern at the best of times, but since he had told her to drop the Fellowes thing, he had been permanently frosty. When the footage finished playing, he yanked out the USB, inspected the Sandhurst photo and re-read the e-mails. She could see the disappointment in his eyes.

"This is thin, Flint. Very thin. What you've got here tells me that, apparently, the man tipped to be the next Chinese VP liked a bit of cock while he was at Sandhurst. I accept this is a possible motive for blackmail. But the rest? Flint, you're a promising detective. Your case record's been on the right side of satisfactory, but since your friend crashed his car, you've been erratic, to say the least." He exhaled, shaking his head. "I mean, first you go upsetting the Fellowes' family – as if they haven't suffered enough. And now you're on about political assassinations?"

She was trying not to look angry, but it was welling up inside her. "I just think it's a possible scenario. At the very least, sir, if someone's blackmailing the Chinese, don't you think we should get off our arses and do something about it?"

His disappointment turned to displeasure. "Careful, Flint, you're on thin ice as it is. What do you want? Pre-emptive arrests?"

She snorted. "It's not like you haven't done it before."

"I'll pretend I didn't hear that. And another thing: who really

174

gives a shit if someone's got the dirty on a Chinese politician? It might even get this country a better deal."

She cut him a deadpan look. He stared back.

He exhaled, puffing out his cheeks. "Right, Flint. Against my better judgement, I'm going to let you go to Whitehall. When the Chinese delegation get back on their plane without incident, I won't rub your nose in it, but I will consider the matter closed. For good." He flicked a finger towards the door. "Off you go. I'll let the Diplomatic Protection Service know you're coming. Be back here Wednesday morning."

"Thank you, sir," she said, with a lopsided smile. She spun on her heel.

"Oh, and Flint?"

"Yes."

"Try not to make a nuisance of yourself."

* * *

Andrew sat in the ward, hogging the TV, glued to a news channel. His fingers tapped the table nervously. An old man complained. Andrew ignored him.

* * *

Jess pressed her way through the crowds chanting *Free Tibet*, flashed her ID at the gates, and was buzzed into Downing Street. She let herself into the guardhouse and casually leaned on the desk. "Alright, lads? How's tricks?"

The three DPS officers eyed her up and down.

She smiled warmly and cocked her chin towards Number Ten. "All them Chinese in there then?"

"Yeah, been there since early this morning," said one.

"Look, lads, I've been sent here from Wembley. We've had information about the Chinese."

The officers were stony-faced. Jess glanced over her shoulder and leaned in dramatically.

"We reckon someone's going to take a shot at the VP. Maybe a bomb, we're not sure."

"News to me," said an officer. "Don't worry, nobody's getting in there. Place's locked tighter than a nun's… Well, tight."

The others snickered. Jess rolled her eyes.

"What's the schedule for the Chinese, then?" she asked, smiling. "Where they off to next?"

A paper was consulted. "Here all day, then a unit to the Dorchester – that's where they're stayin' – and another to Buck Palace."

"Buckingham Palace?" she knitted her brow. "What for?"

"Search me. All I know is we've got to give the escort."

"Alright," she said, making notes. "What about tomorrow?"

"Olympic Village, Tower of London, Heathrow, and home."

"What're they doing in the Olympic Park?"

He shrugged. "We don't get the details."

"Kissin' arses and wastin' time," said another.

"Alright. Cheers, lads." She flashed them her best grin. "Mind if I have a look around?"

"Not a chance, love. You're not on the list." He tapped a computer screen. "No clearance."

She scribbled three names on a pad. "Are they on the list?"

"Sorry, love," he said, without looking.

"So, can I speak to whoever's in command here?"

"That'd be me," said the officer, looking exasperated. "Look, I was told you'd be coming to ask a few questions. That's all. There's not a whiff of anything on the airwaves, and believe me, if the powers that be had any reason to suspect somebody was going to assassinate a Chinky politician, we'd have shooters, dogs, and squads all over the place. Alright? As it is, standard procedure's being followed, so you don't 'ave to worry your pretty little head about it," he said in a patronising tone.

She wanted to smack him. And Barlow. Fuckers. She took a breath. "Well, can one of you escort me up to the back gates?" she said, twirling her ponytail.

The youngest of the three jumped up. He led Jess along the street and past the Prime Minister's residence, while desperately attempting small talk. She nodded and smiled mechanically, her thoughts miles away. They passed a group of reporters, chatting and waiting. There were three cameramen leaning against the wall, bored, smoking.

"They're all accredited and cleared," said her escort, eagerly.

She flicked her eyes all around her until they reached the railings at the end of the street. The heavy iron gate buzzed and clicked open as they approached. Jess hopped down the steps and walked past the checkpoint. She stood on Horseguards Road, hands on hips, fuming.

Placard-brandishing demonstrators filed past, roaring and shouting. The police kept them moving. Nobody was allowed to loiter near Downing Street.

She turned a full circle, examining the trees and the high wall that enclosed Downing Street gardens. She had to admit, it was virtually a fortress. Sighing, she set off towards Horseguards Parade and the National Police Memorial. The distinctive, hulking form of a Maybach prowled the road towards her. She eyed the silver vehicle and the number plate made her freeze. SST RM 1. It glided past her and turned left onto Birdcage Walk.

Fuck, she thought. What now?

She called Andrew and blurted it all out.

"How am I supposed to get this done? That fucking Barlow. No doubt he told them to humour me and send me on my way. They're staying at the Dorchester. Schedule says they're going to the Olympic Park tomorrow, followed by a Tower of London visit."

"What's your gut telling you, Jess?"

"Forget about Buckingham Palace. No way anything goes down there, and I can't see them trying anything at the hotel." She sucked air between her teeth. "If I wanted to take him out, I'd do it somewhere public and blame it on a terrorist. Olympic Park fits the bill; it's a big place. I'll get there early and see what I can see."

"Is that guy still tailing you?"

"Haven't seen him. Maybe they've called him off."

"Jess, I feel so bloody useless."

"What're you going to do?"

"I don't know. *Something.*"

"You just get the all-clear from the doctor tomorrow. That's what you need to do."

"Hmmm."

"Alright, see you."

"Wait! Um, Jess, look, whatever happens tomorrow. I mean, even if they kill Guo, I just want you to stay safe. I don't want to lose you, OK?"

She smiled, her face a deep crimson. For a second she forgot all about Charles and Guo. "Thanks, Andrew. Don't worry about me. I know how to look after myself."

Indeed she did, but Charles and Rupert had a private army.

* * *

Guo's car swept through the gates of Buckingham Palace. He admired the building as the car entered the courtyard.

"Tell me again who we are dining with?" he said to his aide.

"His Royal Highness, Prince Freddie, second son of The Queen. He is a business ambassador for Britain. Business Secretary Grounding will be there, along with a selection of cabinet ministers."

"I suppose we will have to eat their awful food." Guo sighed and ran a hand over his smooth hair. He regretted not bringing Ling with him. Ling would be more at ease with the endless protocols of British Royalty. They ground to a halt, his door was opened, and he stepped out, hoping the evening would not be too painful.

Chapter 30

Tuesday morning, June 19th

There was hardly a policeman in sight when Jess pulled off Loop Road and into the shadow of the massive stadium. She abandoned her car near a western entrance and waved her ID at a flustered security guard.

"You expecting any visitors today?" she asked him.

He shook his head, looking stunned. "Nah, not as far as I know."

Jess wondered how far that was.

She returned to her car and used the radio, her stomach doing somersaults.

* * *

Andrew had packed his bag. His scan was booked for nine-thirty, but he checked his watch every minute. Where was Jess? He resisted the urge to call her, and settled for the TV news channel. The airwaves were buzzing with details of the trade agreement and what it would mean for Britain in a time of recession. Optimism abounded, underscored by a vague mention of growing human rights demonstrations. At least they hadn't got to Guo yet.

Andrew's disposable buzzed. He dashed out to the corridor and pressed it to his ear.

"What's going on, Jess?"

"Andrew, I fucked up. Big time."

He started to sweat. "What? Tell me."

"He's not at the Olympic Park. The schedule's changed. I had to get on the blower and call in a few favours, but I know where Guo Qingling's going today."

Andrew remained silent.

"He's meeting the Queen at Windsor Castle and going to Ascot Races in a royal carriage."

Andrew went pale, then dropped the phone.

When he picked it up, Jess was saying, "If they make it look like a terror attack, it'll work."

He returned to the ward and looked at the screen, thinking back to Piers' e-mail. *Monk lovers.* "Not a terror attack, Jess. They'll blame it on the anti-China demonstrators."

"Oh God. I have to admit, it's perfect."

"Yeah, and who'll profit next year when the Ascot Authority wants to hire a private security force for the week? Probably Slipstream. We've got to get there, Jess. Both of us. You get on the road, warn your comrades, find Charles and Rupert. I'll call Brookson. I've no choice now. I'll meet you at the races. Keep your phone with you."

"And how d'you think you're going to get to Ascot?"

"I've got an idea. We'll keep in touch."

He went to his room, shut the door, and stared out the window. How does one reach a Prime Minister? How did Charles usually do it? He decided the mobile number was a safer bet and would not pose the challenge of getting past an operator.

He dialled. Three times. Turned off.

Sweating now, he took a deep breath and called Downing Street.

"Yes, hello. Good morning," said Andrew. "This is Charles Buckham. I need to speak to the Prime Minister."

"I'll just see, sir. What is it regarding?"

Andrew winced, he hadn't thought of that. "Oh, um, it's urgent. You could say it's a matter of life and death." He could hear fingers strumming a keyboard. He'd probably gone too far. "Please hold, sir."

Several minutes later, he was informed that the Prime Minister would be on the line momentarily. He thanked the operator.

A few seconds later, a crisp voice boomed, "Charlie! I was wondering when I'd hear from you. That Tote thing went smooth as silk."

Andrew cleared his throat loudly. "Good morning, Prime Minister. I'm calling with regard to Charles Buckham, Rupert Calcott, and Piers Bartholomew."

"Who is this?"

He considered lying, but there seemed little point. "My name is Andrew Dixon. I work for Charles."

"Why didn't he call me himself?"

"He's, er, indisposed."

"Look, you'll have to be quick. I've got a very full day."

"Sir, is there any way you can stop the sale of the Tote?"

"What do you mean? It's signed and sealed. Oh bugger, don't tell me there's a problem with the money. Is that it?" he cursed. "And Charlie doesn't have the guts to tell me himself. Put him on the line, please."

Andrew rubbed his temple. He hadn't really thought this through. How do you tell the nation's leader something like this? He cleared his throat again. "Sir, he's not here, and it's not about the money. It's far more serious than that. Deadly serious."

A pause. "Go on." The tone was cautious.

"Charles, Rupert and Piers are planning something awful, which will cause a diplomatic catastrophe and de-rail the trade agreement."

The line was silent.

"Are you still there, Mr. Brookson?"

"I'm listening. What are they planning?"

He took a deep breath. Time to go for it. "They're going to assassinate Guo Qingling. Today, at Royal Ascot. They want Ling Jiao to be the next President, so he'll change the gambling laws to let them broadcast British racing on mainland China."

"Now, look here, I know Charlie's a sly old dog, but what you're saying is positively ridiculous."

"It's not. They've got Ling Jiao in their pockets. They're blackmailing him, I've seen the evidence. It's of a sexual nature."

He told Eddie about the footage.

"Oh come on," he scoffed. Then a pause. "Wait a second, you said your name was Andrew Dixon?"

"That's right."

"Are you Jacko Dixon's son?"

"Yes."

"Huh, well according to the papers, you're as bad as your father. Now look here, you're never to call this number again, do you hear?"

"But—"

"Good morning." The line went dead.

That went well. Shit. He dashed to the main ward, found a paper, and checked the runners and riders for the afternoon.

* * *

Eddie sat back in his chair and stared at the telephone. He wondered if Charlie was telling him everything. He switched his gaze to the painting of Margaret Thatcher above the fireplace. "What do you think, old girl?" he muttered.

* * *

The silver Maybach stood alone in car park one at Ascot racecourse. It was a grassy, tree-dotted scantuary, which usually turned into a large picnic party before and after racing. Spaces here were coveted, and it was not unusual for families to pass them from generation to generation. That was how Piers had got his. Rupert had paid £200,000 to persuade an impoverished dowager to part with her berth. The gang of three parked here every year and used the discreet entrance by the Royal Enclosure garden. "Let the plebs and celebs use the main gate," Piers loved to say.

Rupert reclined in the back seat of his car, reading the paper until the others arrived. His phone rang.

"Eddie! Well done yesterday. Your approval ratings are up since the announcement."

"Thanks, Rupe. I couldn't be happier." A pause. "As long as nothing upsets the apple cart before Guo leaves the country."

Rupert narrowed his cold eyes and raised the divider between him and Goran. "What are you getting at?"

"Is Charlie with you?"

Rupert glanced around the car park. "Not yet. Oh, wait." He spied Piers' car sliding to a halt under a tree. "He's just arrived. I'll put him on."

Rupert marched to the car as Charles and Piers got out. Rupert mouthed Eddie and proffered the device.

"Morning, Eddie. Congratulations. A great coup for British business."

"Hmm. Yes, quite."

"You sound rather serious. What's wrong?"

"You've got the money for the Tote purchase, I take it? No problem there?"

"Not in the slightest, Eddie. Why would you even ask?" A knowing smirk cracked his face. "If it's a present you want..."

"No, it isn't," he snapped. "Charlie, remember you promised me you'd never do anything to mess up the big picture?"

"Of course, of course."

"Well, I just had a surprise phone call from one of your employees – Jacko Dixon's son, to be precise – and he was spouting wild theories about you chaps and the Chinese."

"Oh dear. Sorry about that, Eddie. The poor chap hasn't been right since he crashed his car. Hit his head rather hard, you know. And then there's the drugs. Anyway, what sort of theories?"

Eddie told him. Charles curled his hand into a fist, but forced himself to laugh. "Eddie, you've made my day! I'm most terribly sorry you had to listen to that. It'll never happen again, I assure you."

"To be quite honest, Charlie, blackmail sounds very you, but if your leverage gets Britain the simulcast rights, then I'm inclined to not to give a damn. However, I don't believe you'd have the gall to start knocking off future heads of state. At least, you'd better not."

"Eddie, I'm offended," he replied, smiling. "Who do you think I am?"

"Don't get too big for your boots, Charlie." He hung up.

Charles tossed the device at Rupert. "Get on to your people. I want updates on Flint and Dixon."

A few other cars pulled in nearby. Charles sneered and checked his watch. "Ten-thirty. Let's go before the whole world turns up." He tapped the driver's window of Piers' car. Victor and Felix got out and stood erect, hulking frames filling their black tailcoats. Goran prowled over to join them.

Charles eyed them up and down, checking their ties and waistcoats. "Well, you look the part." He turned to Piers. "Call Draycott, tell him we're coming in."

Piers nodded. Rupert led his soldiers to the Maybach, opened the boot, and gave them a case of wine each.

"Oh, would you?" said Piers, into his phone. "That's awfully kind of you. I'd hate to cause a scene and embarrass the gate stewards." He ended the call. "Good to go, men!"

The six men made their way to the small entrance gate. A few more vehicles arrived, and wives and servants began setting up elaborate luncheons out of car boots. The clouds parted and the summer sun shone down.

Goran sniffed the air. "Not a breath of wind," he muttered. "Excellent."

At the gate, Charles and Rupert strode through, showing their Royal Enclosure badges. Piers stepped up, brandished his, and told the gateman, "These three men are with me," cocking a thumb towards the men with the cases of wine.

"I'm sorry, sir. Not without tickets," said the gate steward.

Piers gave the man his jolliest smile. "I just spoke to your boss, he's–" He noticed Alan Draycott, Ascot's Chief Operating Officer, scuttling towards them, doffing his top hat.

"Ah, there you are, Alan."

Charles eyed Draycott as if he were an insect, and found it highly amusing how the man fawned over Piers.

"Good morning, Sir Piers," he gushed. "How are you?"

Piers shook his hand. "Actually, I'm in a bit of a pickle. Got a chap joining us for lunch today who'll only drink '82 Chateau Cheval Blanc, and the last time I looked, it wasn't on the lunch menu here."

"Oh dear," said Draycott, looking slightly panicked.

"Not to worry," said Piers, waving dismissively. "I brought a few cases with me. As you can see."

Draycott inspected the wooden boxes held by Goran, Felix and Victor.

"These chaps are just going to drop them up to my box, decant a few, and be on their way. I hope that's not a problem?"

"For a Steward of the Jockey Club, nothing is a problem," said Draycott, wringing his hands.

"Wonderful," said Piers, ushering the men inside.

"But, I'm afraid Nigel here," he gestured to the gateman, "and the policeman will, um, have to check the boxes. Standard practice these days; we even check women's handbags. I'm sure you understand."

Charles cut Piers an impatient glare.

Piers kept smiling. "Not at all, Alan. Check away."

The men placed the heavy boxes carefully on the inspection table and prised off the lids. Draycott ogled the expensive bottles longingly. Rupert and Piers exchanged knowing looks. Charles nodded his approval.

"Alan," said Piers, selecting a bottle. "Here's a little something for being so understanding, and one for you – Nigel, was it? And you, Officer?"

The policeman refused. Draycott's eyes stood out on stalks. "I'm quite overcome. I don't know what to say. Thank you so much."

Nigel looked at his bottle as if he didn't understand all the fuss.

"No. Thank you," said Piers. "I won't forget this."

Draycott scurried off with his treasure, and the three ex-soldiers made for the grandstand, minions in tow.

Policemen stood around in bored groups while caterers wheeled tall trolleys of food to and fro. The whole place was calm before the storm of 70,000 racegoers surged through the gates for six days of racing, eating and drinking. There were 247 private viewing boxes in the grandstand. They would be packed all week, and 170,000 bottles of champagne, 160,000 pints of beer, and 10,000 lobsters, would help everyone have a right royal time.

Piers looked about as he walked. He felt nostalgic for the Royal Meeting. He remembered his childhood years when the old grandstand had a kind of dilapidated charm and his father had been Her Majesty's Representative. Nowadays, it was overcrowded and corporate. Still, he thought, can't stop progress. Of course, in a few hours, everything would change once again.

"Bloody hell, Piers," said Rupert. "I thought Draycott was going to offer you oral pleasure."

Piers laughed. "I daresay he would if I asked. He's angling for Jockey Club membership."

"Will he get it?" asked Rupert.

Piers shrugged. "Oh, you know how it is. These things can go either way!"

They all laughed.

Piers had a private box on level two of the grandstand. They entered, placed the wine crates behind the bar, and dismissed the waiting staff with a wad of notes. Goran told Felix and Victor to stand guard outside as he set to work removing the bottles.

Charles and Piers leaned on the balcony. "What time will the demonstrators crank it up at the main entrance?" said Charles.

"Should be starting already."

Charles grinned. "That'll keep the police stressed." He turned on the wall-mounted TV and channel-hopped until he saw the headline: *Chinese VP to Ascot*. "Perfect. Absolutely perfect."

Rupert stood over Goran and watched him empty the cases and open their false bottoms. Goran threw a towel on the floor and pulled on thin silk gloves. He assembled the AS-Val, strapped the knife to his leg, and placed a small pistol and roll of tape in his pocket. Lastly, he secured the rifle under his arm and buttoned his coat.

Rupert pinned a press badge to his lapel and gave him two more for the others. "Right, you know what to do," he said, looking the Serb in the eye. "Keep in radio contact. Wait for my order. Three shots, quick and clean. Leave the gun, flush the gloves in a loo, and get yourself back to the car."

Goran nodded and turned to the door.

"Oh, and one more thing," said Rupert.

Goran stopped.

"If you pull this off, you'll vanish like the man on the grassy knoll. But if you fuck it up, or God forbid, shoot a Royal," Rupert jabbed a finger at his soldier, "I'll turn you into Lee Harvey fucking Oswald. Understand?"

Goran nodded again and disappeared.

"You sure about leaving the weapon on show?" asked Piers.

"The beauty of using such an old piece, is its ubiquity on the black market. Easy for an extremist lunatic to get hold of," said Rupert, winking.

Piers chuckled loudly.

* * *

Andrew left his new phone in his bedside locker and jumped in the taxi. His final scan would have to wait.

On the way to Brockford, he called Susan on the disposable. He thanked her for her concern and said he would be back to work next week. "Oh, and Susan? Did my Ascot tickets arrive?"

"All your post is piled on your desk."

"Good. I'll be with you in forty-five minutes."

"Good Lord!"

The nurse informed Dr. Wilson that his patient was missing. "He took his things, but forgot his phone," she said. "What do you want me to do?"

Wilson tut-tutted, shaking his head. "Idiot. He needs that scan to get the all-clear. Call Thetford police station, ask for Sergeant Hardy, and let him know. That's all we can do."

Traffic was already at a crawl eleven miles from Ascot, on the leafy suburban road. Jess swore and slammed her palm off the steering wheel. She called Andrew; line busy. What was he doing? She inched her car forward and checked her watch: ten past twelve. The royal procession would enter the racecourse at precisely two.

She checked her mirrors: no sign of a man on a Ducati. For now.

She advanced another six feet. Cars ahead started beeping.

Frustrated, she ran her eyes over a sprawling house set in a canopy of mature oaks. There was a mountain bike leaning against a tree. She pulled onto the footpath, locked the car, and made for the bike. She rolled up her trouser suit and swung her leg over. A pang of guilt attacked her. She pulled a crumpled fifty out of her wallet and left it under a stone. As she cycled up the road, she chucked her phone in the back of a pick-up coming against her. That should confuse the fuckers. She gritted her teeth, clicked the gears, and flashed past the carloads of expensively dressed racegoers.

* * *

Rupert's phone buzzed. He listened intently and hung up. When he joined Charles and Piers on the balcony, his face was dark with malice.

"They've ditched their phones, but it's safe to assume Flint's on her way here. Andrew left his at the hospital."

"What do you mean, left his at the hospital?" said Charles.

"He's done a runner. I knew we should've done her in," snapped Rupert.

Charles thought for a moment. "Right, send their photos to your men and tell Felix to grab her when she arrives. Where the fuck is Dixon?"

* * *

The helicopter touched down on the front lawn at Brockford. Andrew rushed through the rotorwash and climbed aboard.

Thierry greeted him with a firm handshake. As the chopper took off, Andrew thought he saw a police car pull up outside the mansion.

"My friend!" said Thierry. "So how are you?" He inspected Andrew. "You're looking a bit pale. You'll have to come to Deauville for some sun. Oh, forgive me. Do you know each other?" Thierry gestured to the couple sitting opposite.

Andrew smiled and shook hands. "Hi Paulie, you're odds-on for the Queen Anne Stakes today."

"Yeah, mate, should be a steerin' job," said Paulie, with a mischievous grin.

"Honor, good to see you again."

Lady Honor Fowler cracked a stiff smile.

Champion jockey Paulie Rockford was about to ride at his first Ascot as retained jockey to Sheik Marwan Al Wahal. Paulie was the poster boy for British racing, his bubbly personality and penchant for dating fashion models had earned him the nickname *Paulie Rock'n'Roll*. Arriving by chopper was standard fare for Paulie and only added to his image. Honor Fowler was his latest conquest, much to her father's disgust.

"What's goin' on, Andrew?" asked Paulie.

"You don't want to know."

"You've had a rough go of it lately."

"Tell me about it." Andrew looked directly at Thierry. "You don't believe what the papers say, do you?"

Thierry looked offended. "Of course not, Andrew. We are friends. I know you too well to believe gossip," he shrugged. "Even if I did, who cares what a man smokes or puts up his nose in his own time? This business is tough on all of us. A man has to have his release."

Andrew was astonished.

Paulie burst out laughing. Thierry cut him a sideways glance. "As long as he doesn't fail a test, eh Paulie?" The jockey went quiet. Paulie's rock and roll lifestyle had once earned him a lengthy ban and almost ruined his career.

Andrew put on his tie and waistcoat as they thumped through the clear sky. "What time'll we arrive?" he asked.

"One fifty-five touchdown, mate," said Paulie.

Andrew winced. It was going to be tight. His head was throbbing again. He called Jess on the disposable.

Felix loitered by the entrance. He could hear the demonstrators outside, chanting *Free Tibet*, and the cries of police moving them away from the busy turnstiles. People were arriving in droves. Streams of brightly-coloured ladies broke up the monotony of black morning suits and top hats. He hoped an on-duty detective would stick out in this crowd. And she did. He saw her show her

ID to the gate steward and march in. She looked a sweaty mess, like a waitress late for work. The copper at the gates nodded and shrugged when she spoke to him.

She made for the grandstand, dodging through the smiling, chattering crowd.

Felix fell in behind her.

Her disposable rang.

To Andrew's relief, Jess answered immediately.

"How's it going?" he asked.

"Bloody hell, Andrew, talk about a needle in a haystack."

"You need to check the private boxes," he bellowed above the noise of the chopper. "Try level two, that's where Piers has his. It's very close to the Royal Box. I'll be there soon."

"Yeah, I'm in the elevator now." A crackle and a muffled shriek.

"Jess?"

"You stay the fuck away from Ascot if you want to see her again," said a whispered voice.

The colour drained from Andrew. He stared at his phone, feeling utterly helpless.

"What are you looking for?" said Thierry.

"Me? Oh, er, nothing. It's just, you heard the Chinese VP's in the Royal procession?"

"It was on the morning news. Why?"

"I have to meet him, that's all."

Thierry arched his brow quizzically. "Brockford expanding into China?"

Andrew exhaled. "Something like that."

He prayed Jess wasn't collateral damage.

Chapter 31

U p on level seven, Felix and Goran stared at Jess. She was awake, sitting on the floor. Her mouth, wrists and ankles were taped. Her eyes burned with anger. She flexed, squirmed and growled.

"She's fucking strong," said Felix. "You sure that tape'll hold her?"

Without a word, Goran grabbed the tazer and zapped her again, long and hard. She shuddered and went limp.

"Go back to ground level and watch out for Dixon. Tell Victor to stay on the door," said Goran.

"What about her?"

"I'll ask the boss. Now go."

Rupert spoke into his earpiece. "Oh that's a bonus, Goran. Tell you what, let's make her the patsy."

Charles nodded approvingly, a smile cracking his face. Piers shook his head.

"Erratic, emotional copper with political issues murders Chinese VP. That sort of thing… Goran, when you're done, break her neck, put her prints on the weapon and throw her down the stairwell. Right, five minutes till go. Wait for the order. Over." He turned to Charles. "You were right not to do her in last week. She's found her niche."

Piers looked doubtful. "It'll drive Dixon over the edge."

Rupert cut him a frosty stare. "Fuck Dixon."

"Yes, you leave him to me, Piers." Charles got up, grabbed his

191

binoculars, and went to the balcony with Rupert. Piers glanced at the door, suddenly feeling uneasy.

"Oh look," said Charles. "There's Marwan's chopper. Christ, it's an eyesore."

Rupert whipped his binoculars around to the infield. The black and gold machine touched down like a wasp beside the other helicopters.

"Thierry's on the pig's back with those Qataris…" Rupert froze. "Jesus fucking Christ." He touched his earpiece.

* * *

Paulie scurried across the heath with Andrew in tow. Red-faced, t-shirted picnickers screamed and yelped at them. *Go on, Paulie. Nice one, mate. Rock'n'roll, Paulie. Any winners, Paulie?*

Behind them, Thierry escorted Honor at a more sedate pace.

Andrew and Paulie arrived at the track crossing. The bowler-hatted steward, sweating in his green velvet coat, waved them across with a grin. Paulie darted into the grandstand, straight to the weighroom. Andrew put on his top hat and ran his eyes along the vast structure. Balconies, seats, and viewing areas were filling up in eager anticipation of the Royal procession. Excited conversation filled the air. People waved miniature flags and snapped photos. The atmosphere crackled; the week was about to officially commence. Andrew showed his badge and was admitted to the lawn. He dodged through the throng, darting his eyes along the rows of private boxes. Six floors. On the second floor, his gaze came to rest on familiar figures.

Goran pulled on his gloves, slid the window open, and peered down. The excited hum of the crowd hit him; he wouldn't be seen or heard. He looked down on them with contempt. He was about to give them an unforgettable afternoon. He set up a metre from the window. Weapon in hand, he leaned on the table and trained his sights on the final furlong marker. He relaxed and slowed his breathing to a zen-like tranquility. Ready. He threw a sideways glance at the bitch in the corner. She was still slumped, unconscious.

There was a crackle in his ear. "Felix, where the fuck are you?"

bellowed Rupert. "He's on the lawn, staring at us!"

Goran ignored the shouts. When the line went silent, he whispered, "In position, ready. Awaiting order."

"Stand by," replied Rupert.

Rupert focused on the elaborate wrought-iron gates at the end of the straight mile. Two stewards in green livery heaved them open. In a few minutes, the carriages would appear and trundle serenely up the straight.

Andrew made eye contact with Charles. Charles dragged a finger across his throat. Andrew darted across the lawn, but a meaty hand snaked out and grabbed him.

The barrel-chested man held his arm like a vice. Andrew saw the tazer and panicked. "Help! Help!" he roared. "I'm being mugged!"

A young couple turned to face him. The large man looked murderous, but he let go, stuffing the tazer in his coat.

"He's a lunatic!" said Andrew, as other people stared at them.

"What's going on?" said someone.

Andrew noticed the large man wore a press badge: he had seventh floor access. Andrew ducked into the sea of top hats. The large man dashed after him.

A cheer went up as the four carriages passed majestically through the gates. Each open landau was pulled by four horses and carried four passengers. A pair of ornately-dressed footmen sat behind the occupants. The whole procession was flanked by two scarlet-clad outriders on white steeds.

Piers found the spectacle breathtaking, as did everyone present, and indeed, most of the nation. Millions were watching on TV. Piers felt a pang of shame. They were about to taint this world-famous, noble summer gathering with blood and fear. Suddenly, he wondered if they had gone too far. He screwed up his face. Nothing could stop it now.

Rupert spoke into his earpiece. "Goran. He's in the second carriage. This side, facing away from you, opposite Prince Freddie and his wife... They'll be in range at the one furlong marker."

"I'm surprised he's not in the Queen's carriage. That's a bit of a snub," said Piers.

"I'm rather glad," said Charles, glued to his binoculars. "We won't get blood on the old dear's dress."

Piers cringed at the thought.

Andrew's hat toppled off as he sprinted through the teeming concourse, barely making it to an elevator as the doors slid closed. Inside, sweaty, breathless and hatless, he was met with disapproving looks. His head pounded. Everyone poured out on the fourth floor, leaving him alone up to the sixth. Then he jumped out and sprinted up the stairs to the seventh.

The seventh floor corridor stretched out in either direction; he checked left, then right. There were officials and journalists milling about and doors slamming as everyone took their places to watch the Queen's party arrive. To the right, at the far end, Andrew saw another brute of a man, standing by a door like a sentinel. Andrew walked towards him, breaking into a run as the man braced himself for a fight. The man raised his fists, a tazer clamped in one. Andrew sprinted.

More loud cheers echoed as the procession passed the two furlong pole. On the Royal Enclosure lawn, the band prepared to strike up "God Save The Queen".

Focused, Goran let out a steady breath and moistened his lips. He had Guo's head in the crosshairs, soon it would be splattered on Prince Freddie's lap. A hundred metres to go. "Ready to fire," he whispered.

"On my mark," came the reply.

He eased his finger over the trigger.

Beside him, the bitch groaned.

At the last moment, Andrew dropped to his knees and felt the air move as a thick fist skimmed his hair. Andrew drove a fist into the man's groin. The big guy doubled over, cupping himself. Andrew hopped to his feet, wrenched the tazer free and jammed it into the man's neck. He keeled over. Andrew kept it in place until a dark patch appeared between the fallen soldier's legs. Checking the tazer, he braced himself and made for the door.

Guo's carriage passed the final furlong pole. The band launched into the national anthem. Goran was in another world, where only him and his target existed.

He heard "Fire at will" in his ear. There was a noise behind him. He would kill the bitch after the Chinaman.

Andrew burst through the door, saw Jess wriggling on the floor, and a man leaning over a table. He darted, thrusting the tazer.

Goran let air leak out of his lungs and gently squeezed the trigger. A sharp pain cut through his side. The shot went high. There was a puff of grass as the bullet bit into the turf. Goran's muscles spasmed, his teeth clenched. Then it was over. He stood and whipped around.

To Andrew's horror, the tazer died. The man swung the gun at him. It was Rupert's driver, the guy from the restaurant. Andrew heard Jess' muffled screams, and primal instinct flooded over him. This man was not going to kill them. He grabbed the gun, forcing the barrel upwards. Another shot cut into the ceiling. Andrew swiped at the man's face, missed, and received the rifle butt in his stomach.

* * *

On level two, the three ex-soldiers watched with horror as the carriages disappeared under the grandstand.

"Bollocks," said Rupert. "Come on, Charlie, I knew we'd need more than three men."

Charles pursed his lips. "When you want a job done properly," he muttered.

"Victor, Felix. State your positions," said Rupert.

No answer.

"Repeat. State your positions."

"Felix here. Number four stairwell. Over."

"Where's Victor?"

"Level seven."

"Right, you go ready my car. We'll meet you there in ten minutes."

"Copy that."

Rupert opened the cases and produced the two spare pistols,

handing one to Charles. "We're a weapon short," he said to Piers.

"Don't worry about me, chaps. You go on. I'll tidy up here, " he replied.

Charles and Rupert made for number two stairwell and bounded up to the seventh floor.

Piers put the wine cases back together, replaced the bottles, and casually walked away from his box. He took the lift to ground level and hustled his bulk to car park one. He would have to drive himself home.

* * *

"Fuck you!" roared Andrew in a deep, primitive voice. He drove a knee into the man's groin and followed with a throat jab. The man fell backwards onto Jess, a pistol spun across the floor. Ankles taped, Jess looped her legs around his neck, clamping her thighs against his head. He dropped the rifle, pulled a knife, and drove it into her leg. She growled, her eyes bulging. Andrew dived for the pistol, jammed it into the man's torso and fired twice.

The man went limp, blood leaked onto the floor. Pistol in one hand, Andrew pulled the knife out of Jess and cut her restraints. She ripped the tape from her mouth. They stared at each other. Breathless.

Andrew heard a movement behind him.

"Stand up and turn around, Dixon," said Charles, slowly entering the room.

Andrew froze. He dropped the pistol in Jess' lap. She tucked it under her jacket.

"You heard him, Dixon," said Rupert, closing the door.

Andrew got to his feet and turned, the bloody knife in his hand. Rupert aimed his weapon at Andrew, a two-handed grip. "Charlie, if you'd told me this morning that your little dog would be the end of Goran, I'd have laughed."

"So would I, old chap." Charles edged over to the window and looked out. "Drop the knife and pull that chair over here, Dixon."

The knife fell onto Goran's body. Andrew sidled over with the chair, flicking his eyes between Charles and Rupert. His heart was pounding. Rupert trained his gun on Jess. Charles aimed at Andrew.

"Good. Put it by the window," said Charles.

Andrew set the chair down.

"Now get on it and jump out. Or I'll be forced to shoot you in the head."

"Don't you dare, Buckham," roared Jess. "You're not going to do us like you did Fellowes and the Turk."

"Shut up, bitch," spat Rupert.

"Catherine Fellowes?" said Charles in a calm voice, keeping his eyes on Andrew. "Huh! She wanted to take away my income. And this from a billionaire, whose family pay no tax anywhere. Ha! No wonder George was lost without her; the money was all hers! As for Yildiz? He was just a man who tried to back out of a fifteen million pound deal. Needs must, Dixon. Needs must. After the accident, his replacement was happy to go ahead; he even told me the deal would honour Okan's memory!"

Andrew threw his hand around the room. "You don't seriously think killing us will clear this mess up, do you?" he said. "Your man is dead." He pointed at Goran's body. "The police are going to figure it out. You'll go to jail this time." He shot a glance at Rupert. "You too, arsehole."

Charles curled his lips into a crooked smile. "I used to enjoy your naivety, Dixon. It made you easier to brainwash. Now I just find it fucking boring." He stood and thrust the gun into Andrew's stomach. "Nobody'll figure out anything except what *we* want figured out. Understand?"

Andrew shook his head mockingly. "You're on another planet."

"You know what Napoleon used to say, Dixon?" Charles leaned closer. Andrew could smell wine on his breath.

"I'm sure you're about to tell me."

"*History is a set of lies agreed upon.* And let's face it, he should've known," he chuckled. "Nobody wants to hear the truth if it's ugly. They prefer simple, convenient lies. So, when we tell them that–"

"Oh, shut the fuck up, you vain prick," Jess snapped. "I'm sick of your bullshit."

Charles shot a look at Jess. "Pretty face, filthy mouth."

Andrew seized his chance. In one fluid movement, he grabbed the pistol, forced it to the ground and smashed his forehead into Charles' temple. Charles squawked. The gun went off. Andrew screamed. Glass shattered.

Rupert, surprised, took his eyes off Jess. Big mistake. She brought up her pistol and emptied the magazine into his chest. Below, people in the stand started screaming.

Andrew, seeing stars and regretting his headbutt, tried to wrench the gun from Charles, but the pain in his leg was intense. The two men fell to the floor, grappling, struggling.

Jess tried to stand, but her leg gave way, blood seeping into her trousers.

Charles rolled over, taking the upper hand. He pinned Andrew underneath him and started pummelling his head. Pain ripped through Andrew. He was losing clarity. He couldn't even block the blows.

Suddenly, Charles stopped, a confused look contorted his features. He stood, twisting, grabbing at his back. His fingers found the knife, buried to the hilt between his ribs. Jess stood behind him, triumphant.

"You fucking bitch!" he said, yanking it out.

"Go to hell," she roared, half-falling, half-pushing him.

He staggered, lost his footing, and disappeared over the edge.

Jess collapsed beside Andrew. He was barely conscious.

Out on the stand, she could hear frantic screams. She fumbled for her disposable.

Epilogue

Friday, June 22nd

Jess hauled herself out of bed and clicked out to the kitchen on her crutches. Her father was making breakfast. "You look much better. Eggs?" he said.

"Yes please, Dad." She eased herself into a chair and checked the time. "I was out for fourteen hours."

"Mmm. You should, er, read the paper," he said.

She picked up the broadsheet and read the headline: *ROYAL TERROR AT ASCOT*. She rolled her eyes and read on.

On the Royal Meeting's opening day, a lone gunman gained access to Ascot racecourse with plans to assassinate a member of the Royal family. The man, identified as Serbian immigrant Goran Vlasic, posed as a journalist. Vlasic, who had radical tendencies, was fired from his position at Slipstream International several months ago when he refused psychiatric counselling and was deemed unfit to carry out his duties. Police are not ruling out links to Al-Qaeda.

Vlasic died from injuries sustained during the desperate skirmish to subdue him. Tragically, two other men were also killed. The casualties were Slipstream International CEO Rupert Calcott and the Hon. Charles Buckham, a stud farm owner and former soldier who served in Iraq in 1991. Both were enjoying a day at the races when they found themselves dragged into the tragic events. Detective Sergeant Jessica Flint, who apprehended Vlasic, was also injured.

Paying tribute to Mr. Calcott, the Prime Minister said that his tragic death "was proof of Rupert's heroism and devotion to his country". Both Calcott and Buckham are to receive posthumous honours for bravery in defence of the Monarch. Detective Flint will also be honoured.

In an official statement, Slipstream International expressed shock at the awful turn of events and said that although Mr. Vlasic was unstable, their assessors and observers had no reason to believe he would carry out such an attack.

Following the death of its founder and CEO, Slipstream International will merge with Minotaur Securities.

In a separate statement, Minotaur indicated that a thorough assessment of all personnel would be carried out, in an effort to ensure such a tragedy could never happen again.

Tuesday's racing was cancelled, but the rest of the week is proceeding as planned. The Queen did not alter her schedule and is in attendance, as normal, for the remainder of the meeting.

The Ascot Authority has promised an immediate and full review of their security measures.

Her mouth hung open. She chucked the paper on the floor in disgust. "What a load of crap. A fucking award for Buckham?"

Her father shrugged despondently. "Whatcha gonna do? You got your man. Relax, go with it."

She tucked into her breakfast, lost in thought. "Take me to the station after this?" she asked, between bites.

As she clicked through the office, she was met with cheers and whoops. She barged past them without stopping or cracking a smile, and made for DCI Barlow's office.

He stood and extended a hand. "Well done, Flint."

She produced the newspaper and threw it on his desk. "Have you read this fucking bullshit?"

Barlow's face darkened. "Ditch the attitude, Flint. You've got two months' paid medical leave and you'll probably get an OBE."

God, she wanted to punch the spineless little shit.

"And strangely enough," he continued, "we got a match to the prints on that bag of pills found in your boyfriend's car."

"Let me guess: Goran Vlasic."

"Got it in one, Flint. So, don't worry. Your boyfriend'll no doubt avoid jail. If he has a decent lawyer. Oh, and if you keep your gob shut and your head down, it wouldn't surprise me if you made Inspector when you return." He arched his brow expectantly.

"*If* I return," she said, heading for the open door. As she left, the only sound was her crutches on the tiles.

She went straight to the hospital to see Andrew. He was sitting up in bed with a bandaged leg, looking thin and bruised, but he lit up when she hobbled into view.

"We're some pair," she said, giving him a peck on the cheek.

"Scan was clear this morning, but they're chaining me to the bed for a few days' observation."

"D'you see all that rubbish in the papers?"

"Yeah."

"Guys like them always get away with it."

Andrew half-smiled. "Not scot free, though. They *are* dead."

They both burst out laughing.

"What're you going to do for work, now your boss is gone?"

"Funny you should say that. Jamie Royston came to see me this morning. He was in great form. He brought Charles with him – in an urn! You know, you did him some favour chucking his brother off the ledge."

Jess shrugged and cut him a lopsided smile.

"He's selling the house and gardens, wants me to stay on and run the stud for him." He sighed. "I told him I couldn't stomach it."

"Attaboy," she grinned. "You'll find something else."

"I suppose. Except my lawyer came to see me yesterday. Looks like I'll still have to face charges."

She smiled. "Well, maybe not. My DCI just told me the prints on the bag of pills matched to Goran."

"You mean they printed a dead man?"

"Of course. Standard practice these days."

Andrew smiled. "I'll call my lawyer."

Jess winked. "I'll handle that, Andrew. I'll call Thetford station, too. It'll be very satisfying!"

Andrew smiled. His heart started thumping. "Um," he began,

looking nervous. "Hey Jess, when I'm out of here, do you fancy going out for dinner?"

"Come to my place and we'll share a pizza," she said coyly.

"No, Jess, I mean a restaurant. Somewhere nice." He looked deep in her eyes. "A date."

She beamed. He kissed her.

"Where d'you have in mind?" she said.

"Anywhere but The Scimitar!"

Downing Street. A week later

The Prime Minister closed the file, drummed his fingers on the desk, and picked up the phone. "Send him in please, Miranda."

The door opened and Piers entered. "Morning, Eddie, old chap," he said, with a nervous smile.

"Sit down. And knock off the '*old chap*' shit. Those days are over."

"Yes, Prime Minister."

"I called you here because I'm counting on you to honour the conditions laid out in the sale of the Tote," he said arching his brow.

"Oh, er, um, well—"

Eddie cut him off. "You'll assume chairmanship and announce an injection of forty million into prize money for the next three seasons and you *will not* make anyone redundant."

Piers nearly choked. "There simply isn't the cash for that."

Eddie shot him a hard stare. "Find it. Call it a personal donation. You could sell your shares in Slipstream after it merges with Minotaur. Or you could just write a cheque," he shrugged. "I don't really care where the money comes from, but you'll do it if you want to keep your nose clean. Anyway, Minotaur have said they'll keep renting your land as a base, so you'll make the money back sooner or later."

Piers opened his mouth as if to complain, then exhaled, nodded and said, "Yes, Prime Minister."

"What? Not a thank you? You should be grateful I've thrown you a bone."

"Oh, I am, Eddie. I am."

Eddie stood and went to the sofa. He sat and patted the cushion beside him. Piers reluctantly moved.

Eddie leaned close and whispered. "How bloody *dare* you abuse our friendship and jeopardise Sino-British relations with your little stunt. And if you ever think of taking revenge on Jacko Dixon's son or that copper, I'll ruin you. You'll go to jail and your family'll never live it down." He slapped Piers on the knee. "What about that, *old chap*?"

Piers nodded, coughing.

"Oh, and one more thing. When they examined Vlasic's body, they took his prints. You'll never guess where they threw up a match." He cocked his brow at Piers.

Piers' jaw hung open. There was panic in his eyes.

"On the bag of ecstasy pills found in Andrew Dixon's car. How on earth could *that* have happened, *old chap*?"

Piers spluttered.

"His lawyer is delighted, but if Dixon has to appear in court, this whole fucking mess could come out."

Piers' throat was dry.

"I'll have to make sure the charges are dropped. That's another one you'll owe me."

Piers nodded slowly, his features pale.

"That'll be all for now," said Eddie.

Piers staggered to the door.

Beijing - A month later

Guo and Ling stood at the window of the tall building watching the sun set over the capital.

"I heard that your friends died that day at Ascot races," said Guo. "Apparently, they stopped a terrorist from assassinating the Queen." He shot a quick glance at Ling. "I am very glad I was not sharing her carriage that day. I might have become what they call 'collateral damage'."

Ling kept his eyes on the orange orb as it sank behind the

horizon. "I heard about that also. It is very sad. But, personally, I am just glad you returned safely."

Guo pursed his lips. A long pause ensued. Eventually, he checked his watch. "I won't be able to stay for dinner. I have something else to attend to," he said.

Ling nodded slowly.

"Oh, and I think it would be prudent for you make sure all your affairs are in order. I am authorising an oversight committee to investigate corruption in the whole party. They will look into every nook and cranny. I would hate for them to find anything to hold against you, Comrade Ling."

Ling nodded, flashing his toothy grin. He hesitated a beat too long. "They are welcome to audit my affairs at any time."

"Good," said Guo, already making for the elevator.

Ling remained at the window. He sighed. Another decade of waiting.

He wondered what happened to the video of him and Jamie, he could rest easier if he had the original. Maybe he should send someone to find it. Discreetly, of course.

* * *

When she saw the front page, Jess bought the *Racing Post* for the first time.

DIXON TO TRAIN FOR MARWAN AL WAHAL, read the headline. *In a surprise move which stunned the racing world, former point-to-point trainer Andrew Dixon – son of disgraced banker Jacko – has been signed to become a private trainer to the Qatari Sheik next season. "Andrew is an exceptional horseman," said Thierry Lefleur, racing manager to Sheik Marwan. "We are delighted to have him on the team. His dedication to his charges is reflected by his insistence that he will train no more than fifty horses at a time."*

She grinned. This time, they were reporting the truth.

ABOUT E.H. WARD

E.H. Ward was born in England in 1973 to a racehorse trainer father and a mother who studied speech and drama at the Royal Academy in London. He moved to his mother's native Limerick in Ireland at the age of nine and grew up riding, pony clubbing, fox-hunting, and working for local racehorse trainers and stud farms.

After school and a brief stint in the British army, he returned to England to start full-time work with racehorses. He spent the '90s travelling the world working with horses and in the bloodstock industry. From England, he moved back to Ireland then down to the Hunter Valley in Australia where he worked on a large stud farm and travelled and spent time on a cattle farm, breaking-in wild horses.

From Australia it was on to Kentucky the home of American horse racing and breeding, where he began working for the US arm of Ireland's renowned Coolmore Stud. He spent the next ten years working at Coolmore and was put in charge of their China/Mongolia project, spending six months creating a stud on the plains of Inner Mongolia and a year training racehorses on the outskirts of Beijing.

He was seconded to the Turkish Jockey Club for a year to upgrade and run the Turkish National Stud, before returning full-time to Ireland in 2001, as an area manager at Coolmore's Tipperary headquarters.

In 2006 he went back to Turkey to build and manage a racing/breeding operation on the Aegean coast working with a local businessman who wanted an international standard manager/advisor.

He is married to a Frenchwoman, and they have one son aged five. He currently divides his time between the stud farm near Izmir and southern France. He writes analytical articles and horseracing and sale reviews for The Irish Field newspaper and James Underwood's Racing and Breeding Digest in the UK.

Find E.H. Ward online

Facebook
https://www.facebook.com/EHWardhorsewriter

Tirgearr Publishing
http://www.tirgearrpublishing.com/authors/Ward_EH

OTHER BOOKS BY E.H. WARD

A Sure Thing
Released: April 2014

Irish stud farm manager and bloodstock expert, Oliver McMahon, is tired of his life, and a boss who neither rewards, satisfies, or recognises his abilities. He turns to his very wealthy brother, Richard, for help in setting up his own venture, only to be rejected and, in the process, discovers a family secret.

On the brink of despair, Oliver remembers and calls in a favour owed to him by a man who has risen to become one of America's most powerful mafioso. Oliver gets back on track with a rich client, a large budget, top class horses, and an old flame rekindled.

As the Thoroughbreds start winning, Oliver reconnects with his college sweetheart and all his dreams are being realized. Soon, he's pulled into a tangled web of narcotics, murder, deceit, and sinister threats.

When Richard is murdered, Oliver has to face the awful truth that a decade-old act started the chain of events which led to his brother's killing.

Oliver has no choice but to become as ruthless as Richard if he's to extricate himself from a lose-lose situation. Death or a lifetime in prison – the stakes have never been higher.

Lightning Source UK Ltd.
Milton Keynes UK
UKOW06f0916100315

247605UK00013B/257/P